SWINGERS

MARNIE VINGE

YELLOW TRUCK MEDIA, LLC

Copyright © 2023 by Marnie Vinge

All rights reserved.

No part of this book may be reproduced in any form or by any electronic or mechanical means, including information storage and retrieval systems, without written permission from the author, except for the use of brief quotations in a book review.

Editor: Collette Carmon

Ebook ISBN: 979-8-9880918-2-0

Paperback ISBN: 979-8-9880918-3-7

www.marniewritesthrillers.com

For all you ghouls that like it dark and twisty

ONE

MY BEST FRIEND Jackie recommended we install color changing light bulbs in the pool. As her husband backs me into the softly glowing lavender water and kisses me, I have to say she was right.

I sink down until the warm water is touching my chin. Nathan, Jackie's husband, does the same. He's tall, but not as tall as my husband, Billy. Not as slim, either. Built like an MMA heavyweight fighter, Nathan is far stockier than my husband. Billy is built more like a track or basketball star. A funny thing to my ex-husband, Michael, who is also built like a track or basketball star.

My hands are pink in the lavender glow. Nathan reaches for me and pulls me across his knee, into his lap. Where Billy's hands are smooth, Nathan's are rough. Billy spends his days working as a financial advisor at his own firm. Nathan is a mechanic.

For now, though, it's just me, Nathan, and the fireflies.

Mid-July in Texas means lightning bugs everywhere,

their little bioluminescent bellies pulsating a yellow-green in the night air, streaking slowly across backyards in suburbia.

It would be romantic. But this isn't really about romance.

Tonight, I'm hosting a party. Billy, in one of his sour moods, isn't taking part. He's buried deep in his work inside his home office, doors shut so he doesn't invite any unwanted socialization. Besides myself and Billy, there are three other couples here. Jackie and Nathan are one of them.

Nathan kisses me again and his hand trails down between my thighs. I look over his shoulder as Jackie rounds the corner out into the backyard and I flash her the widest, most wicked smile. She mirrors it and gives me a wave of her fingers.

They're delicate and long, punctuated at the end with nails sharp enough to kill a man. All except two of her fingers. Eight stiletto acrylics and two that are short and oval. Painted all black, she calls these her party nails.

Jackie steps to the edge of the pool and shimmies out of a pair of shorts that look like they might be airbrushed onto her body. Frayed at the edges and worn in like a favorite denim jacket, they hug her curves effortlessly. She has an hourglass figure, the kind that society would have most women kill themselves to achieve. But Jackie comes by it naturally.

Beneath the shorts, she wears her bikini bottoms. Black with short and wide metal pyramids decorating the places where the strings tie together. Her top is much the same, barely covering her breasts. Despite the heat, her nipples are hard beneath the fabric.

She tosses her hair over her shoulder as she joins us in the water. Jackie's hair is shaved on one side, long on the other, and just as dark as her manicure. Smokey eyes and pouty red lips complete the look. She's a bombshell.

She's younger than me by about seven years, only twenty-four. She seems like a kid in some ways and so mature in others. Billy hired her two years ago, and that's how she met Nathan. One afternoon, Billy sent her to take his car to have the oil changed and Nathan was the mechanic on duty. Sparks flew. Happily ever after and all that.

Jackie walks up and kisses the back of my shoulder. She works her way up my neck and I reach for her, finding the soft velvety texture of the shaved side of her skull. And then she kisses me, her tongue just as soft and velvety against my own.

I forget about Nathan, drifting into her arms. She pulls me close. Nathan makes some noise of encouragement in the background, but he's not even there to me anymore. Jackie smells like cherries and vanilla ice cream. Her kiss tastes like sweet mint. She reaches for the strings of my bikini and pulls slowly at one of them until the whole thing comes undone. She does the same to the string around my neck and I let the top fall.

I look into her eyes. And for a moment, this might not only be about sex; it might be about romance.

She backs me toward the deep end, dark as midnight because we haven't changed out those burned-out bulbs for the new ones yet. A husky chuckle escapes her throat.

The water swallows me up, climbing my body like mercury climbing a thermometer.

The way Jackie looks back at me, I think she might think the same thing.

We never talk about it. It's like an enormous elephant listening in on every conversation we have with each other, but neither of us will address it. We're married. To men.

Swinging isn't about love or romance. Friendship, maybe. Swinging, to me, is about sexual freedom and expression. About the way it feels to look into your partner's eyes while they fuck someone else, knowing the whole time they're putting on a show for you. It's about not being afraid to share your partner, confident knowing where they'll lay their head at night. I've never wanted to be truly monogamous. Yet, somehow, I've married monogamous men. Twice. And just like my first marriage, this one is about to fail as well.

Jackie kisses me again, this time needfully. She sighs when our mouths connect. I press my body against hers, our feet barely touching the slope into the deep end. I feel her hands all over me, snaking further and further towards the center of my body.

"Y'all," Nathan says. His voice is faraway. It barely registers. It's like Jackie and I were two passengers on a capsized boat, now huddling together beneath the upside down vessel. Nathan's voice comes from somewhere outside of that cocoon.

"Y'all," he repeats.

Jackie pulls away from me. I don't want her to. She turns to Nathan, annoyance on her face.

"What?" she asks.

"What is that?" Nathan asks, pointing at something behind us. He stands up out of the water to get a better look.

Jackie turns her head and as I'm following her gaze, something bumps into my shoulder. It's weighty, solid. I turn and reach for it, wondering what the hell my teenage daughter put in the pool before she went to her dad's house.

When my hand makes contact, I know on some level what it is. Fabric, skin. An arm. A human.

I whip around, my toes barely touching the bottom of the pool. It floats closer, up into the lavender glow of the new lights.

I see the side of his face, bruised and looking like a center cut filet. Bright pink.

It's Billy. Fully clothed, floating face down in the pool.

And I think he's dead.

TWO

"BILLY!" I shout, jostling the body that floats in our pool. I flip him over and it takes more effort than you'd think, giving a new meaning to dead weight.

Face up, he looks even worse.

"Help!" I shout at Nathan. Jackie is already around on Billy's other side, ready to pull him out of the pool. Nathan quickly lurches toward us and grabs Billy underneath both his arms.

He drags him to the steps and out of the pool, grunting and gritting his teeth as he pulls his friend out of the water, across the concrete and onto the grass.

"Get Jason!" Nathan shouts at me.

Jason, now a music teacher, was a volunteer firefighter. He knows CPR.

Jackie wraps an arm around me and hurries me into the house, both of us dripping wet and immediately saturating the carpet just beyond the patio. The burgundy textile looks a deep bloody red as we hover there. Jackie grabs a towel for me from the patio and wraps me in it. I look down at my feet, the water from the pool spreading out further and further, bleeding more and more into the fibers of the carpet, turning it almost black. And it's right about then that I feel funny. A little detached from the moment, like I'm outside of my body, floating above it, observing.

Jackie helps me over to the couch.

"Jason!" she shouts out behind herself.

The house is in the mid-century style, all one floor. The sound of her voice seems to boom off into every corner of the house. It's eerily silent.

Just then, Jason and Amanda come out of the hallway that leads to Olivia's room, Billy's office, and the game room. From the opposite hallway come Dan and Nicole. Each man with the other's wife. Nicole looks at Jason for reassurance.

Jackie's frantic as she tells them what's going on. Billy, outside, not breathing, needs help, come quick. Jason goes to him. Nicole watches her husband head out to the pool and touches her hand to her mouth in shock. She looks the way I imagine her to look when one of her kindergarten students does something inappropriate. For what she was just doing with another woman's husband, Nicole has an innocence about her.

"What happened?" Amanda asks. She went to all the right private schools and got into Harvard, though she didn't go. She met Dan the summer she turned eighteen and sacrificed Harvard for him. Dan is classically handsome, looking like a 1940s or 50s movie star, even on his worst days. The two of them look like money and both work at high-paying jobs.

"We found Billy in the pool," Jackie says to Amanda.

Dan runs a hand through his prematurely silver hair.

"Is he alright?" he asks.

I feel numb. I don't know if my husband is alright, and there's a part of me that doesn't care. A part of me that hates him. Has hated him for a long time now. Billy changed after I married him. Still, this is shocking. Not at all how I imagined it would end.

"We don't know," Jackie says, pulling me tighter, protectively, against her. I can feel the warmth of her skin through the towel.

"What do we do?" Nicole asks.

"Just wait," Jackie instructs her.

For her youth, Jackie knows how to take control of a situation. It comforts me she's stepping up.

"Call 911!" Nathan shouts from the patio, poking his head in through the back door as he does so. There's a frantic look on his face. Eyes wide with panic. He's such a big guy—someone I don't imagine is afraid of anything—and he looks terrified.

Jackie lets her arm fall from around me and gets up to get her purse. She plucks out her phone and dials the emergency number. I rock myself slowly, wondering if all of this is a dream. Or perhaps a nightmare. Nicole takes Jackie's seat beside me. She wraps an arm around me, but where Jackie's felt strong, Nicole's feels weak.

She's used to comforting five-year-olds with skinned knees, not women who just found their husbands dead in the pool.

"Hi, we need EMTs as soon as possible," Jackie says

into the phone. She walks into the dining room, out of earshot, for the rest of the call.

"Are you okay?" Nicole asks me.

I look at her for a moment, wondering if she knows exactly how stupid that question is right now. Would she be okay? But I just stare at her blankly, without the energy to tell her how I really feel.

From outside, I hear Jason's voice.

"Come on, man, stay with me," he says.

The numbness I felt moments ago spreads, and once more I find myself outside of my body, looking down on the scene as if I'm reading it third person in a novel. I sit on the couch, towel wrapped around me, and I've stopped rocking. Nicole meekly rubs my back, almost like she's afraid that she's going to make me mad. It's irritating, but the emotion is distant. Dan and Amanda stand in the entry hall, Dan's arms crossed and his jaw set. I wonder if he's trying to show Amanda that everything's okay. But Amanda doesn't seem to need such comfort. Her face is set, steely. There's a flicker of something in her eyes, and I struggle to identify it. Maybe the practice of years being Dan's rock. She's immune from the chaos.

Jackie emerges from the kitchen and comes back, displacing Nicole on the sofa. I'm grateful. She instantly wraps her arm firmly around me, and I lean into the embrace.

"They're on their way," she says to all of us.

I can still hear a commotion outside. I wonder how long it will be before one of the guys comes to the conclusion that Billy's not going to wake up.

I saw him in the pool.

He's dead, and everyone who's seen him knows it.

From my vantage point above everything, I look down on myself.

I'm the picture of calm. Or, maybe, the picture of shock. Tears don't streak my face. I'm not hysterical. I'm silent, leaning against my best friend as she holds me and rubs my back. The contact of her palm against my shoulder blade grounds me, keeps me from floating away. I fear that if she stops, I might disappear into the ether and never return.

Suddenly, I hear the siren. It's distant, probably a half mile away. It draws closer and Nicole goes to the front door to watch for it. I hear it getting louder and louder and think about all the times that I've heard an ambulance coming and never thought twice about it. Never gave a second thought to who it might come for and why.

I don't think I'll ever hear one again without wondering and worrying about the people who called it, and the person who needs it.

"They're almost here," Jackie assures me.

I feel nothing still. But then a dawning realization comes over me. I think about Billy's reputation as a financial advisor. About his legacy. I think about how that would impact my daughter Olivia if people knew what kind of party we were having here tonight.

It would ruin Nicole and Jason, both of them elementary teachers.

The gossip mill would chew Dan and Amanda up, working in the same skyscraper downtown.

Jackie's already without a job now that Billy is gone. I can't imagine how she'd find more work.

The conclusion is obvious and I don't know why I didn't come to it immediately.

The ambulance is right out front. The siren cuts off. They're here.

I know what I need to say.

I speak for the first time in quite a long time.

"Everyone listen to me," I say. My voice is hoarse, like I've been silently screaming since I found Billy. Everyone stops and faces me. I see concern on their features. They know what I'm about to say, but I still have to say it.

I take a deep breath.

"This was just a regular party. If they suspect anything else, Billy won't be the only one without a future."

THREE

AMANDA ANSWERS the door and points to the back patio, saying something I can't quite hear. Two young EMTs carrying all the equipment they might need come through the door, marching through the living room and out into the backyard. They don't waste any time.

Billy's dead. I know this in my gut. I saw him in the pool. His face looked like someone had hammered it with a meat tenderizer. I see his face again, bruises beginning to bloom across it. There's no way Billy was conscious when he hit the water.

What happened?

I look around the room. These people are our friends. Aren't they?

I try to assuage the guilt I feel for not being devastated. Billy wasn't the nicest to me.

When we got married, he thought the fact that I wanted to swing was cool and fun and different. After watching me fuck someone else's husband, he thought differently. He especially thought differently when he saw me fuck someone else's wife.

When he realized that swinging wouldn't be about him, the switch flipped.

Billy thought this was going to be centered on *his* pleasure, as most men who get introduced to the lifestyle do. He didn't count on the fact that this was what I wanted. That swinging was what broke up my first marriage, bless Michael's heart.

Billy didn't count on the fact that I was my own person with my own wants and needs.

That really pissed him off.

I'd asked him if he wanted me to quit after he stopped participating. He stopped shortly after realizing just how much I enjoy it and how unbothered I was by the idea of him sleeping with someone else.

He'd always tell me no, go ahead, do your thing. But there was resentment there.

There was judgment.

I sort of walked around in constant fear that he'd bring a priest to the house to exorcise me one day. But now that day would never come. Now I'm out of the marriage I've wanted out of for a long time.

I don't know how to feel about that. And I hope it's not something that the EMTs can pick up on. Suddenly, I find myself back in the fifth grade, stealing AirHeads from the 7-11 and hoping the cashier can't read minds.

So far, I haven't found that to be a big problem in life.

Fingers crossed, tonight will be par for the course.

One of the EMTs comes quickly back inside, looking

serious. I feel nothing. My stomach doesn't plummet. I don't slap a hand to my mouth in horror. I don't cry.

"Are you Mrs. Karlsen?" the older of the two asks me.

"Yes," I manage.

"We're taking your husband to the hospital. You're free to ride with us or follow in your car. The police will meet you there," he tells me.

I nod back at him.

"Okay," I say, mostly to myself. "I need to go," I tell Jackie. She nods.

"We'll drive you," she insists.

I nod and go grab my clothes.

AT THE HOSPITAL, they put us in a waiting room. It's not the regular emergency room waiting area. This one is for people who are about to receive bad news. You can feel in it the air, the thickness of grief hanging around us.

Amanda crosses her arms and gives Dan a look. Whatever was written on her face earlier is replaced with something else: concern. Dan shares a glance with her briefly, and then looks away.

This isn't good.

Nicole and Jason sit on the loveseat across the room, and he squeezes her leg to comfort her.

She doesn't look comforted at all.

Nathan stands by the door, arms folded. And Jackie still sits next to me, arm wrapped around my shoulders. I'm grateful for that, even if I'm not the classically grieving widow.

Widow.

Not a word I'd ever thought I'd use to describe myself. But here we are.

No one says anything. The silence and tension in the room builds, getting thick enough that you could slice off a corner with piano wire.

I look around at everyone. All of them are uncomfortable. Except for Jackie. I don't sense that from her. Nathan looks almost checked out. I don't blame him. He was there in the pool.

But something is dawning on me.

The group of us. Seven without Billy.

We were the only ones here tonight.

Stop.

This has to be an accident.

Billy knew how to swim, but he was fully clothed when he got into the pool. Or maybe fell into the pool. He'd been drinking a lot lately. Like a lot.

Could he have gotten blackout drunk in his office and stumbled out the pair of doors that lead onto the other side of the yard? Did he make his way to the poorly lit deep end of the pool and wasn't able to see where he was going? Could he have fallen in and not been able to get himself out?

It's the only rational explanation.

These people are our friends.

Before I can think too much about that, a young doctor opens the door of the waiting room. Her eyes find mine like there's a beacon drawing her to me. I don't know how she senses it, but it's clear she knows I'm the person she's looking for.

"Mrs. Karlsen?" she asks softly.

I nod.

"I am so sorry. We did everything we could."

IT'S NOT long before the police show up.

Immediately, one of them zeroes in on me. Maybe it's the look on my face. Maybe it's because Jackie's got her arm around me. I don't know. But he makes his way over to me.

"Mrs. Karlsen?" he verifies.

"That's me," I tell him.

"I'm so sorry to hear about your husband," he goes on. "There are officers at the scene and we'll be out of your hair soon."

"Of course," I say.

I nod and thank him. He and the other officer head out into the hall together. I wonder how many calls like this they get.

Man in his early forties dies at home. Probably more than you'd think.

Once again, the rest of us are left in the thickening silence.

I think about earlier today, when the group chat I'm in with Amanda, Jackie, and Nicole was intensely active, all of us messaging each other back to back at the same time. Lots of laughing emojis. Plans for the evening. Who was bringing what to drink, what to snack on.

Now I feel like I'm in a room with people I don't even know.

How do I talk to them now?

I tell myself that I don't have to figure that out right this second.

Things move fast and slow at the same time. I hear one cop on his radio outside. Finally, they come back into the waiting room, but their demeanor is different. Not as friendly. Something's off.

"Due to the nature of the scene, we're going to have someone else come and look at it," the senior officer says. "They're processing it right now."

I furrow my brow.

"What do you mean?" I ask.

"It's normal, when someone passes like this," he assures me. But there's none of the comfort in his voice that was there before. "In a situation like this, we need someone else to take a look at it. Just a precaution, ma'am."

He says it all so easily. My husband is gone. Someone *else* needs to look at the scene. After a moment, I come back to myself. I want to tell him we don't need precautions. Billy had an accident. That's all there is to it.

But I'm not sure he'll listen to me. I don't think that's how this works.

It all happens quickly. Someone else arrives, this man in a suit. He's handsome, probably early thirties like me. He's got blonde hair and blue eyes that pierce whatever stands in front of them. I feel it immediately when his gaze lands on me. He walks over and speaks to me like there's no one else in the room.

"You're Kimberly Karlsen, am I correct?" he asks. He has a strong Texas drawl.

"You are," I tell him.

"My name is Detective Underwood, but you can call me Troy," he says. "I'm just here to go over what happened tonight and make sure that there's nothing else that needs to be investigated."

I furrow my brow, only for a second.

"Okay," I say and nod.

He steps outside with one officer, and they're gone for a few minutes.

Jackie squeezes my shoulder and leans in to whisper in my ear.

"It's gonna be okay, Kimmie," she says.

She's the only one that uses that nickname. Or at least the only one that I allow to get away with it. It's not my favorite, but there's something playful in the way she says it. Right now, it reminds me of normalcy.

Underwood—Troy—comes back in.

"Would it be alright if I spoke to you alone, Mrs. Karlsen?" His tone is utter politeness, but there's something wolfish about him. Like a predator seeking prey. And it's not lost on me he finds the scene suspicious. If I'm being honest with myself, I would, too, were I in his shoes and didn't know any of us.

I stand up, wrapping my jacket tight around me.

"Let's go out in the hall," he says.

And then he takes the lead.

I follow him out into the hallway. The thick walls muffle the sounds of the emergency room around us, obscured in this little pocket for the grieving.

"What can you tell me about what happened tonight?" Underwood asks.

"We were having a party," I say. "And my friends and I were in the pool when we realized Billy was floating in the deep end. We pulled him out and he wasn't breathing," I say, thinking that a short answer is far better than one that's long and drawn out. But the look on Underwood's face tells me he finds it suspicious.

Maybe he doesn't expect a recently widowed woman to be so put together.

"I see," he says. "And where was everyone else?" he asks.

"Umm," I stumble. "Dan and Amanda were inside. So were Nicole and Jason. We went to get Jason because he knows CPR," I tell him.

My heart beats faster in my chest, realizing that none of us took the time to get our stories straight. Who knows what anyone else will say and how it might contradict the picture I'm painting of the night?

I try to calm myself and inhale deeply.

"One of the cops noticed a bikini in the pool. Do you always swim in the nude with your friends, Mrs. Karlsen?" Underwood's eyes trail down to the tops of my breasts in my tank top.

"It's a nice night," I tell him, feeling myself bristle at the questioning.

Underwood is onto us. Or at least thinks he's onto something. Whether he knows the truth, I'm not sure. But he seems like a smart guy, observant. It's probably only a matter of time before he figures out that we were having a swingers' party tonight. The thought devastates me.

It especially devastates me for Olivia.

I've failed her.

"Are you alright?" Underwood asks.

"Fine," I assure him, gathering myself once again. I wrap the towel so tightly around me I feel like I'm in a cocoon. It makes me feel safe.

"Who did you say you were in the pool with?" Underwood asks.

"My friends, Nathan and Jackie," I tell him.

"And what's the nature of your relationship with Nathan and Jackie?"

I feel like a wounded animal, bleeding in the forest, and I can hear the wolf sniffing, getting closer and closer.

"We're good friends," I tell him.

"Alright," Underwood says, okay with this for now, realizing he's not going to get much else out of me in the way of details. "Well, we're going to take statements from everyone, and your husband will have an autopsy. We'll do toxicology, too," he says. "Standard stuff."

It's almost a threat. Like he knows he's going to find something.

I stiffen.

"Great," I say. "I want to know what happened as much as you do."

Underwood's eyes narrow for the briefest moment. Then he smiles at me, his teeth sharp and white in the moonlight.

"Good," he says. "Glad that we're on the same page."

He steps over to the officers, saying something that makes one of them smirk.

Disgusted, I go back to the waiting room.

FOUR

AFTER UNDERWOOD QUESTIONS NATHAN, it's done.

They've got their statements, and I'm chewing on a hangnail without realizing it. Probably not the best look for someone that wants to portray innocence in the whole affair.

After everything, Nathan and Jackie take me home. Everyone else follows.

A crime scene unit is at the house. It's strange to see them here. They're wrapping up, putting equipment back into their van. They clear out and it's over.

When the CSU people are gone, we go inside.

Underwood has assured us he'll be in touch if he has further questions after the autopsy. He also tells me I'll be able to make funeral arrangements for Billy as soon as they release the body from the Medical Examiner. Again, he assures me, standard stuff.

It all seems so strange. So foreign. Once again, I float

in the third person, watching it all happen like it's a TV show and I'm just some viewer at home.

This is someone else's life and nothing I need to get worked up over.

But I know the reality.

It's my life.

And I don't think that fact has fully sunken in yet.

I wait for the last police car to back out of the driveway before I turn my focus away from the front yard. They're all gone. I lean against the wood and breathe a sigh of relief. I'm glad that it's done.

At least that part.

I open my eyes and see my friends in the living room, not looking much different than they had when the EMTs first got here. Everyone seems shell shocked, a little worse for the wear.

I step to the edge of the living room and fold my arms over my chest.

"Did anyone tell them what we were doing tonight?" I venture. My voice comes out meek, small. It's nothing like I normally sound.

Normally I'm brassy. Bold. Something that Michael loved about me and that Billy hated after a while. But something I couldn't change if I wanted to.

I feel reduced by the events of the night.

"No," Jackie says. Nicole shakes her head.

I nod mine.

At least that's out of the way.

"Good," I say. We all know what rides on that and why we couldn't be honest about our lifestyle. Dallas is conservative. You can't swing a dead cat without hitting six churches. Any queerness is a justification for all sorts of unpleasant things. Men who not only like to watch their wife fuck someone else, but might also like to fuck that guy, too? Probably not going to help you land that promotion or keep your job as a teacher. And women who do the same? Good luck.

"Are you alright?" Jackie says, getting up and coming over to me. She takes one of my hands. "This has to be traumatic."

I want to tell her it's probably far less traumatic than she thinks it is.

I haven't been in love with Billy for a while.

Guilt washes over me.

I don't really care that he's dead and I should. A good wife would.

But I didn't love him.

And Billy did everything in his power to make sure that I knew I wasn't shit without him.

The only silver lining was that he got along with Olivia. At least we didn't have that stressor in our household. I don't think I would have stayed if that hadn't been the case.

But I also don't know how willing I was to swallow another divorce.

One divorce is one thing, but a second one? *Here?* This isn't Hollywood. This is a place of hellfire and damnation. The streets reek of brimstone, sulfur. And judgement. Not from God, but from your neighbors.

Everything's bigger in Texas, including the wrath of the self-righteous.

My living room is silent. Jackie wraps me in a hug.

I don't know what to say to anyone. I don't know where we go from here. Am I supposed to make everyone feel better? I feel like they're the ones who should do that for me. But not really, we don't owe each other anything. And I'm fine, other than the shock.

I wonder if tonight is going to be one of those horrible tragedies that marks a before and after in your life. Our friendships might never be the same. I can't imagine all of us together, happy again.

This will always be there in the background. The phantom waiting just offstage.

It's absurd to even think of that right now. What's wrong with me?

I fantasize about my life without Billy. Terror is what I should feel. It should devastate me. But I feel something entirely different.

I feel hope.

Everyone gets their things together and one by one, the couples leave. Jackie and Nathan are the last, and I want to beg Jackie to stay. I don't want to sleep alone tonight.

I feel like this is all my fault.

"You'll be okay?" Jackie asks when they're at the door.

I can't bring myself to ask more of her tonight. She's a good friend. And she's got a life of her own with Nathan, despite whatever may be between us. I feel a pang of sadness when I think about spending the night without her. I want her to stay. But I don't tell her that.

"I'm fine," I tell her. "You guys just go on."

Nathan nods at me, and Jackie's eyes tear up. She wraps me in another embrace.

"You call me," she whispers. "I don't care if it's three in the morning. You call me and I'll be here as fast as I can."

I nod and feel one of her hot tears hit my bare shoulder.

"Thank you," I manage, feeling myself getting choked up now.

She pulls away.

And just like that, they head to their car, their taillights retreating into the night.

FIVE

I SIT on the edge of the bed, still wrapped in the towel from a shower. I needed to be clean. The light is on and the room's too bright. Everything has a sharp edge in my vision. I glance over my shoulder at Billy's side of the bed. I'm surprised when I turn and don't see him there.

I breathe a sigh of relief.

That he's gone for good washes over me. I should feel worse. No dutiful wife would feel glad. I should cry my eyes out, asking God why.

I never would have wished this on Billy. I really just wanted him to leave.

I feel responsible.

Like I put his demise out into the universe and now it's happened.

I get up from the bed and go into the kitchen. I swing the fridge open and the cool air hits my skin. Refreshing, it brings me back to the present. I grab a can of Dr. Pepper that I keep on hand for Olivia and her dad when he's here. I rarely drink them. But suddenly, I want something sugary.

I imagine it's because what I really want right now is a cigarette and I quit two years ago.

Exchanged one vice for another, I suppose.

I take the can into the living room and I sit down on the couch. The surrounding quietness is overbearing. The silence feels thick. Everyone should still be here. When they left, I should've been ready to have a fight with Billy. The house should be anything but quiet.

I drink the Dr. Pepper. When I finish, I lay down on the couch, still only covered in the towel. I fight for sleep for the rest of the night. Finally, just before dawn, it comes within my reach and I seize it.

PUTTING on makeup is the last thing on my mind when I wake up on the couch. Or making myself look anything like I usually do. Instead, I frantically throw on a pair of jeans, a top, and flip-flops. I throw my hair in a messy bun and grab a pair of my biggest shades. Dawn is breaking, and I know this is right around the time that Michael and Olivia like to have breakfast on their Saturday mornings together. If I know either of them at all, they'll be at their favorite restaurant, Hashbrowns. Normally, Michael brings Olivia by after their outing. But today I can't wait for that.

Not bothering to glance at any clock before I leave, I hope that my guesstimate about the time is right. Whatever. It doesn't matter. The only thing on my mind is that I need to tell Olivia what happened.

Or at least tell her that her step-dad is dead.

A knot forms in my stomach as I drive across town. The thought comes back to me about Olivia finding out who I really am. I can't even imagine how horrific the backlash she'd face at school would be. It sends a shudder through me the way scary movies used to on Friday nights when I was a kid.

This is worse, though. Scarier. It's *real*.

I swallow the lump in my throat and my stomach turns. I feel like I'm on a rollercoaster, up and down over the next few miles of my journey. Finally, I get myself to calm down and I turn onto the street where Hashbrowns stands.

I cruise for parking and see Michael's red truck.

I pull into the parking space next to him with my SUV. Then I wait.

People come and go from the building in front of me, and as each person pours out of the door, I both hope and dread that it might be Michael and Olivia.

I don't want to tell her this. I don't want to tell him, either. Even though Michael knows who I am and what I do on the weekends, I don't want to see anything resembling reproach on his features.

Michael and I have remained good friends. I was the one to end our marriage. If I'd let him, Michael would have stayed. He thought the sun shined out of my ass, even if I wasn't really monogamous. Even if I enjoyed sleeping with women as much as men. Even if he had no interest in participating in any of that.

For Michael, it was different. It just wasn't who he was. There wasn't any insecurity about swinging. I just always felt like Michael deserved better than me. He deserved someone who also wanted monogamy. I felt like my lifestyle had to hurt him on some level. Even if Michael wasn't willing to come right out and tell me that.

When we were married, he looked at me like I was the greatest person he knew.

He still looks at me like that.

And I fear that sharing this news with him is going to make him look at me entirely differently. Like somehow, my lifestyle is at the heart of why this happened. That maybe this will be a turning point for him. That he'll see me as I really am.

I really, really don't want that.

And I don't think I realized that fully until I parked and had a moment to think about the situation.

Finally, the two of them come out of the restaurant and I watch as they make their way down the sidewalk to the truck. I roll down my window and wave at Michael. He spots me and a smile breaks out across his face. That'll be short-lived.

"Hey," he says, carrying what I imagine are Olivia's leftovers in a styrofoam box.

Olivia sees me, and she smiles, too.

"Hey, you two," I say.

Olivia examines my face as she comes closer and her brow furrows. I can remember being a kid and sensing when something was wrong with my mom. Olivia has that same ability.

I feel that turning sensation in my stomach again, like

I'm going to be sick. This time, it feels like I might really throw up.

"Hey, can I talk to your dad for a second?" I ask Olivia as they step up outside the SUV.

She looks between us, trying to read what's going on.

I want to tell her she won't guess this one in a million tries.

"Go get some cookies," Michael says, fishing out a ten from his pocket. He gestures over his shoulder at a little cookie boutique down the sidewalk.

Olivia seems wary, like she doesn't want to leave us. She wants to know what we're talking about. There's suspicion in her eyes. But she goes.

"What's up?" Michael asks, a toothpick from the restaurant sticking out of his mouth.

Michael is handsome. Tall, thin. Looks like he could have played basketball in college, even though I know he didn't. He still looks athletic. There's something about him that reminds me of an Ancient Greek olympian that might run the marathon.

I shake my head, struggling to figure out where to start, and then it just pops out of my mouth.

"Billy's dead."

Michael barks out a surprised laugh.

"What?" he asks.

My expression doesn't change. His does, going from startled laughter to seriousness.

"Billy died last night," I tell him. "We found him in the pool."

"We?" Michael asks. "Oh, a party," he adds without judgment. "How many people were there?"

"Seven, not counting Billy," I say.

"What happened to him?"

"He drowned," I say. "I think."

"What do you mean, *you think*?" Michael asks.

"I'm not sure. They're doing an autopsy to find out," I tell him.

"Jesus, are the cops involved?"

"Yeah, they are," I say. "And a detective."

"Christ, Kim," Michael mutters. "That's serious."

He looks at me then in a way that I don't like. Like he's measuring me, gauging my reaction.

"Oh, stop it, Michael. I had nothing to do with this."

A smirk breaks across his face.

"You're full of surprises," he tells me.

There's a softness in his expression that makes me think even if I had been the one to kill Billy, Michael wouldn't fault me for my crime.

He'd probably help me get away with it. His total indifference towards Billy would come in handy, were that the case.

I smile gently back at him. It's nice to have someone like Michael in your corner.

"Do you think someone did something to him?" Michael asks.

I think about the bruises on Billy's face.

"I don't know," I say, but I feel a knot in my stomach.

Like my body is trying to tell me something I'm not ready to hear.

"I guess that's for the Medical Examiner to figure out," I tell him.

Michael makes a noncommittal noise, like maybe, if it

were him, he'd already be jumping to some conclusions about what happened last night. And there's a part of me that follows his logic. A part of me I keep holding back, not wanting to admit that possibility to myself.

I sweep it under the rug in my mind. I'll come back to it later.

"I have to tell Olivia," I say.

"Of course," Michael says.

Just then, our daughter comes walking up the sidewalk with a box full of the best sugar cookies in town.

"Hey, kiddo," I say to her.

She smiles at me.

Olivia is fifteen. A total tomboy like I was at her age. She's quiet, and she does well in school. She's as tall as Michael and she plays basketball. Usually, when she spends the night with her dad, they play video games together. Though Olivia tells me that Michael usually has a bit to drink and falls asleep on the couch before she's done playing.

"There's something your dad and I wanted to tell you," I say to her.

That same worried look comes back, washing over her features in a flash. I get out of the SUV, putting myself on the same ground as her. I reach for her shoulders.

"It's your step-dad," I say. "Billy died last night, Liv."

Olivia's expression remains unchanged, but her jaw sets. And in that instant I feel it. She's turning her upset on me.

We struggle to get along, and Olivia is notoriously stoic about her emotions with people, much the same as me. Michael has always been way better at reading her and relating to her. I can sense the accusation radiating off of her. The thought that I brought this man into her life, she adjusted to him and even liked him. And now he's gone.

She feels like this is my fault for ever bringing him around.

She doesn't have to speak. I can feel her betrayal.

Olivia shoves the cookies into her dad's side, and he takes them. She marches around to the back passenger side of the SUV and climbs in. This is going to be a fun ride home.

I look at Michael and he gives me an expression of sympathy, and I get back into the SUV.

"Liv, take this," he tells her, handing her both the cookies and the to go box, reaching over my head. She takes them without a word.

"Olivia," I say, looking at her in the rearview mirror. "Are you okay?"

"Fine," she says.

The sentence is clipped, like she had to bite it off to even get it out of her mouth. The implication in her tone is that I should know *why*. Again, this is all my fault. I have no intention of taking that away from her. However she needs to get through this, I'm fully supportive of that. Even if that means I'm the bad guy for a while.

"You call me if you need anything at all," Michael says softly to me. He squeezes my hand and I squeeze his back.

"Thank you," I say genuinely. I don't know what I'd do without Michael when it comes to raising Olivia. I couldn't have done it alone, and fortunately for me, Michael is a man that's invested in the raising of his child. Even after our divorce.

Michael steps back from the SUV. He calls to Olivia.

"Call me, kiddo," he says.

"I will, Dad," she says from the backseat. Her tone is less grumpy with him.

"I'll call you when I know anything," I tell Michael.

"Sounds good." He pauses, and then he adds, "Kim, look out for yourself."

I nod.

And then I back the SUV out and turn down the street.

SIX

"I NEED to pick up some things," I tell Olivia when she asks me why we're stopping at the super center on the way home. My thyroid medication is ready and I'm totally out. I wouldn't make her go if it weren't an emergency. "It won't take long. We'll go straight home afterwards." She makes a grumpy noise from the backseat, letting me know she'd rather be anywhere but here right now. Preferably anywhere that I'm not.

I want to tell her tough luck, kid. You're stuck with me.

But I resist the urge.

Besides, nothing feels funny right now and joking seems inappropriate.

I don't know how much Olivia realized about where Billy and I were at with our relationship. I wonder if she had any inclination that we might end up divorced, like me and her dad. I wonder how she might have reacted to that news.

Probably much the same. Maybe even feeling more

like it was my fault than it is that Billy died. And I would have understood. I understand it even now. I just want her to be okay. And I never feel like I'm doing this parenting thing right.

I think most moms feel that way, like they never do enough. They don't sacrifice enough; they don't make the right parenting choices. But most of us are just doing the best we can with what we know in the moment.

Still, I feel I've failed her.

Like Billy's death really is my fault. And the fallout for Olivia is even more my fault.

She liked Billy. They did a lot together. He helped with the basketball team. He was the fun step-dad to her. Too bad he couldn't have been the fun second husband for me. At least he was for a little while. Things changed, though.

"Come on," I tell her after we park and I turn off the engine.

Olivia drags her feet getting out of the SUV. I fight the urge to snap at her and tell her to hurry. But she's fifteen, and the world still revolves around her. And she's also just lost her step-father. I remind myself of that when I get frustrated with her. She needs some grace.

Maybe we both do.

We head into the store. We head for the pharmacy and I get my prescription. Right next to us is the electronics section, and Olivia wanders off into the video games.

I mill around in one aisle and look at the phone cases.

Somehow it feels sacrilegious. Looking at something as frivolous as a phone case when my husband just died.

I think I'm mainly feeling guilty because I wanted out of my marriage with him. Now I got what I wanted, but he's dead.

Any decent wife would have cried by now.

But I'm not a good wife.

That's what I told Michael when I asked him for a divorce. It's what Billy echoed back at me when he told me I was worthless. I wasn't a good wife. So it's probably fitting that I haven't shed a tear for him.

I look at the phone cases but don't touch them. Meandering to the head of the aisle, I look at some books on an end cap. I wonder if I could read right now. My focus is shot. I can't imagine it. I long for the escape that they could provide me, though, and so I throw three into the cart. All thrillers.

I want something that will show me someone has it worse than me right now.

That someone is existing in a hell of their own making and they'll find a way out of it.

Because that's what I feel like I'm in right now. I'm wishing I'd never met Billy. That I'd never married him. If I hadn't, we wouldn't be in this position. I wouldn't be dreading to hear from Detective Underwood about Billy's autopsy results, knowing that whatever he was going to tell me about them would be upsetting. Yet I keep clinging to the idea this was an accident.

All I care about right now is that Olivia ends up being okay.

I walk to the back wall and look for her. I step over to where the video games are and see her browsing. I smile to myself. She needs this sort of normalcy.

Maybe I do, too.

I walk back over to the phone cases and throw in the one I was looking at the most.

And it's right then that I emerge from the aisle and spot Amanda at one of the end caps. I walk her way, but I slow down when I see she's entirely engrossed in what she's doing. She tosses one item, and then another, into her basket. I stop walking; the cart lurching forward with its own momentum.

Before she notices me, she turns and makes a beeline back to the front of the store, leaving me in her dust, unaware of my presence at all.

Curiously, I walk over to the display she was picking from. Several styles of simple cell phones line the end cap. Most of them remind me of phones I had when I was in high school. Flip phones or brick phones with minimal capabilities.

What the hell does Amanda need with these?

Amanda and Dan always have the latest iPhone. While I'm still carrying my iPhone X, the pair of them are always geared up to upgrade to the latest device as soon as it drops. They always have to have the newest and the best of everything. And with the money they make, I imagine I would feel the same way.

Billy hated it when I spent money. He pinched every penny and got me to quit working. So I never went shopping or splurged on anything for myself. The phone case seems like an extravagance. Also, a fuck you to the man I found dead in the pool last night.

That makes me even happier that I tossed it into the basket.

I walk back around to the video games, looking for Olivia. She almost runs into the cart, two video games in hand.

"Can I get both?" she asks.

I feel like it's a challenge, and I immediately yield to her.

"Of course," I say.

She tosses them casually into the basket.

"Is there anything else you need? For school? For fun?" I ask, resorting to buying Olivia's favor. I never said I was perfect.

Olivia shakes her head, not saying anything more.

I nod, and then the two of us head for the front of the store to check out.

And as I do, something dawns on me. An episode of a true crime show that I saw comes back to me, unbidden. I remember the person using prepaid cell phones to communicate where the police wouldn't be able to track their phone calls as easily.

I think about Amanda tossing them into her basket.

SEVEN

I SCAN the parking lot for any sign of Amanda, not wanting to run into her out here. I was careful in the self-checkout, looking at every station, making sure that Amanda wasn't at one of them.

I feel like I was spying on her. But I think she was doing something nefarious. Something that called for spying. I wonder if there's any kind of regulation on phones like that. If it flags the system if someone buys more than one at a time. Somehow I doubt it.

If I've learned anything from true crime, it's that often, the tech available to law enforcement is exaggerated in TV crime dramas. I would be surprised if there were such a system. Likely, Amanda bought those with cash and no one is going to be any the wiser unless they pull the security videos of her buying them. And to do that, they'd need to know when she was here. Without a credit card, that might be difficult.

Jesus, what am I thinking?

As we walk to the car, I feel the weight of someone's eyes on my shoulders.

I turn quickly, not wanting Olivia to be alerted to anything. I don't see anyone, though, except a car with a dark windshield and its headlights on in the bright daylight.

I'm probably being paranoid. Worrying about someone following me because I was following Amanda, sort of.

That's probably all it is.

Or at least that's what I tell myself as I load the groceries into the SUV. Still, I feel a sense of urgency, like prey realizing a predator is stalking them. I look back once again and the car with the headlights and the dark windshield is still just sitting there. Likely, the person inside is waiting for someone or doing something on their phone. Or maybe they're on their lunch break. Maybe they're eating and checking social media.

There are a million things that person could do that have nothing to do with us.

I shut the back door of the SUV and Olivia returns the cart a few spaces down. I watch her the whole time, suddenly feeling overprotective. She comes back unscathed and we get into the car. I buckle my seatbelt and turn the SUV on, then back out. When I shift into drive, I glance once more in my rearview and find a troubling image.

The car has pulled out of its spot and it's beginning to approach, slowly.

I speed up a little too quickly in the row of parking

spaces. I reach the turn out onto the main road and take it a little too fast.

"Mom," Olivia says. "You're driving like a crazy person."

There's disdain in her voice that only a teenager can muster.

"Sorry, sweetie," I say. "I think I'm a little tired."

Olivia says nothing.

I merge onto the highway and notice that the car is still following us. I speed up and it does the same. I slow down and it does the same. Never passing, always keeping pace with us. It makes the hair on the back of my neck stand on end.

Who the hell would follow us?

Billy was a likable guy. He did well for himself in business as a financial advisor. Billy had successfully made many people a lot of money. He'd never mentioned that anyone might be upset with him. But even if they had been, how would they have known where we lived? Or how to get into the house with that many people there?

It's absurd, I tell myself.

The car isn't following us.

I decide to head across town, wanting to test my theory that the car is following us. I get off the highway and head over to a place that Olivia likes to get salads from. It's a trendy little restaurant that mostly caters to the crunchy crowd and athletes like herself.

I turn on the street where the salad restaurant is and I pull into the parking lot. As I do, the car just glides past, like there was never any intention of following us. I breathe a sigh of relief.

I get in line and we order. I pay and take the bag from the teenager who looks like he'd rather be anywhere else but here. And then we turn out into the street.

My chest feels looser, my limbs not strung with tension. I don't grip the steering wheel until my fingers ache. We get on the highway and I stop looking in the rearview mirror for a bit.

"What would you like to do when we get home?" I ask Olivia.

She just grunts. Which probably means that she wants to play video games and for me to leave her alone. I wish I had some of Michael's magic touch in talking to her. But I don't and there's really nothing I can do about it.

We drive on for a few miles and I glance in the rearview. When I do, my stomach sinks.

A black sedan is following us.

I speed up, switch lanes. They do the same.

I slow down, switch lanes again and drive way under the speed limit.

They just keep following behind us.

I tell myself that I'm being paranoid. This is a crazy thing to think. Who would even want to follow us?

But then, when I get off at our exit—the one closest to the house—the car follows us. It turns right, just like we do. And then as soon as we turn into the neighborhood, it just drives past.

I'm left feeling both relieved and immobilized. Worried about the fact that they came this far. There's no way that car wasn't following us home. Who the hell was it? And why?

It makes me think about the party last night. About everyone that was there, and how well I know each of them. I know Jackie best of all. I've let Nicole watch Olivia. Back when she was a preteen.

I keep looking in the rearview mirror as we head to the house, wanting to make sure that the car didn't take one of the other entrances to the neighborhood, snaking and winding through it, making their way to us. For that to happen, they'd need to know us. Or at least know where we lived.

My mind reels. Insanity threatens to creep up behind this intense paranoia.

No one was following us. It could have been two different cars.

I repeat it over and over again in my mind, trying to reassure myself. Olivia, when I look in the rearview mirror, seems none the wiser. Which is how it should be. She's already upset. The last thing she needs is to think her mom is losing it.

But am I losing it?

It was weird that the car followed us as far as it did. I gave it multiple chances to pass us on the highway. And for someone that kept close pace with our SUV, they never wanted to pass. The worst part is that the windows were so tinted that I had a zero chance of even trying to make out who was behind the steering wheel.

It wasn't a car I recognized. Just a black sedan.

No one I know has a black sedan.

That part is the weirdest.

I pull into the driveway and open the garage door. It creeps up slowly, making me will it to hurry somehow. I pull us in and shut it, once again wishing it would close faster, entomb us inside a place of safety. Although, after last night, I don't know that this house will ever feel safe again. Not really.

I look at myself in the rearview mirror. My Jackie O shades swallow up my eyes, hiding any trace of strain that the ride home might have caused me.

I don't know how I'm going to make this right for Olivia, or if there's even any way for me to do that. I can't bring Billy back from the dead. And I'm not sure that if I could, I would.

Isn't it important for kids to see their parents in healthy relationships? More important than shielding them from the inevitable reality of mortality?

I don't know. I wish I could protect Olivia from everything. She's so young, still so innocent. There's so much shit that life is waiting to throw her way in the real world. I wish I could keep her here with me forever so she wouldn't have to learn any of the hard lessons that I had to.

We get out of the car and head inside. Afterwards Olivia disappears into her bedroom. I sigh and stand at the kitchen counter for a moment, surveying the empty and quiet house, wondering what exactly our lives are going to look like going forward.

Billy's money will carry us, I think. Even though he never really had me involved with the finances, Billy made a great deal of money. He was extremely successful. I'll keep the house and Olivia can continue to grow up here.

Or maybe it would be better to move.

Somewhere that her step-father hadn't drowned.

The choices ahead of me feel overwhelming. I haven't even planned Billy's funeral yet.

Then there's a knock at the door.

EIGHT

I JUMP, startled almost out of my skin. My heart races and I stand there for a moment, wondering if I should pretend we aren't home. Wondering if I might get a look at the person at the door without revealing we're inside.

Could it be whoever was following us?

The thought swirls in my mind, like debris picked up by a tornado, trying to find some place to land. I can't shake it. I stand there, paralyzed. Then another knock comes at the door, this one more insistent.

My tongue is a cotton ball, and I struggle to swallow.

I peek out of the kitchen into the entry hall. All I can see is someone's dark silhouette through the frosty glass of the front door.

I think about slipping down the hallway to see who it is, peering out from the game room. But the idea is ludicrous. I'm Kim Karlsen and on a normal day, I don't take shit from anyone. I shake my shoulders and put my chin up.

Whoever it is, I'll deal with them head on.

I head to the front door and grab the handle, pausing for a moment. Then I throw it wide and behind the frosty glass is a face I recognize.

Jackie.

"Oh, God," I breathe a sigh of relief.

"Were you expecting someone else?" she asks.

"Not exactly," I say. "I thought—oh, never mind. Come in."

She steps inside the house and I close the door behind her, checking twice that I've locked it.

"How are you?" she asks abruptly after I turn to face her.

"Well, my husband is dead and my fifteen-year-old seems in shock about it. So great," I give her a sad smile.

"I would expect nothing less," Jackie says with the same expression on her face. "You have any wine?"

"In the fridge," I tell her.

Jackie's a good enough friend that she helps herself and serves me. She knows where the wine glasses are. She knows, of the two bottles of white in the fridge, that I'll prefer the buttery Chardonnay. She even knows which glass is my favorite. A steal from Pottery Barn—a stemless glass resting in a skeletal palm, its fingers stretching up around the vessel.

All these things she seems to know effortlessly.

Billy hadn't known any of them and he hadn't made any attempt to.

Jackie hands me the glass, about two servings full.

I take a sip.

"How are you really?" Jackie asks, her voice soft.

Her full lips are painted a hot pink today that stands

out against her jet black hair. She's in a band t-shirt and cut-off shorts, not as akin to an airbrushed pair as the ones she wore last night.

"I don't know," I tell her. "I feel like I'm floating above it all."

"Isn't that like a classic trauma response?" she asks. "I mean, I took a psychology course at the community college and I swear they talked about that."

I raise an eyebrow at her and smirk. It makes her laugh.

"You're right," she says. "If you need a psychologist, you should probably go to a professional." She chuckles and looks down at her feet. I can see how Nathan fell for her.

Jackie's charming and outgoing. She reminds me of me at a younger age. She speaks her mind without reservation, even when she's alone in her opinion. I hope the world doesn't suck that out of her.

"I'm fine, though, really," I tell her. "It's just weird."

"I get that," Jackie says, as she often does, even though there's no way that she could actually get it. But I admire her unwavering ability to make people feel seen.

"You know, I wished for so long that Billy and I would get a divorce," I say. "I talked to you about it. I wished for it basically every time I laid down at night. That our marriage would be over. I even think I once prayed for it to be over one way or another. But I never wanted this."

"Of course not," Jackie says. "But you weren't happy. And that's not a crime."

"You're right," I say. And she is. It's not a crime to want out of a marriage that's not working.

But in this case, it feels like it is.

"What do you think happened?" Jackie asks.

"I honestly have no idea," I say. "Most of the night is fuzzy for me. The main thing I remember is finding Billy in the pool. I had a good buzz, but finding him sobered me up. Shocked my system, I guess."

She's silent for a moment, seeming to stare off into space.

"You okay?" I ask her.

"I'm fine," she says, smiling at me. "I just—I came over here to mention something to you. About Billy."

My stomach clenches instantly, does a flip-flop, too. I don't want to know anything that's going to come out of Jackie's mouth next. I want to shrink and disappear into some other woman's life.

"Did Billy ever tell you anything about his clients?" she asks.

"No, not really," I say. "Just general things about how it was all going. That sort of thing."

I swallow, dreading whatever she's going to tell me.

"Did you know he managed Dan and Amanda's money?" Jackie asks.

I'm shocked. I had no idea.

"No," I say, unable to find any other words to go with that one.

"I found something you might want to see," Jackie says, then fishes into her tiny pocket. She produces a small yellow sticky note, the top folded over. She hands it to me.

Owe Blankenships $155,000 by Friday

"What the hell is this?" I ask, not really understanding why Jackie's showing it to me.

"I found it in Billy's desk," Jackie says.

I still don't understand. I look up at her, confusion probably written on my features.

"I think he owed them money," she goes on. "Dan and Amanda. They had invested with him. And I think they wanted part of their money back, ASAP." Jackie says.

"What are you saying, Jackie?" I ask her, my voice feeling heavy as it comes out of my throat. I don't like where this is going.

"I'm saying that it's weird, right?" Jackie says. "Dan and Amanda want their money by Friday and then Billy dies. Don't you think that's weird?" she asks.

My head swims.

Could these people that I've known for so long—that I've shared my house and my food and my body with—have done something to Billy?

"I mean, it had to be one of us, right?" Jackie asks.

The thought is one I've been working hard to keep filed into the recesses of my subconscious, but as soon as she speaks it aloud, I know she's right. It had to be one of us here last night. That leaves seven people, eight minus the one that died. And only six if I don't count myself.

I want to tell Jackie this is absurd, that she shouldn't be thinking this way. I look down at the note in my hand again. Why wouldn't he have told me if he was working with the Blankenships?

Also, Billy was doing incredibly well for himself. It

shouldn't have been a problem for him to get the money for them. Why would they kill him before he did that?

I look at the house around us. He had the money. Our lifestyle was proof of that. Olivia went to private school, paid for by Billy. We drove new cars. We had a decorator come and do the house after we bought it. Mid-century had always been my dream. I remember Michael teasing me about it when we got it, saying that it was the house I always wanted that he could never give to me. Billy had me pinch pennies, though. He hated for me to make large purchases out of the blue.

I feel sick.

"So, you're saying that you think they had something to do with what happened last night?" I ask Jackie, point blank.

"I'm just saying that you might want to show that to the detective," she says. "I could be totally wrong, Kimmie, but I have a feeling."

The use of the nickname softens me. I love it when she calls me that. I stare at her for a moment, not because I'm searching her face for anything. Not because I'm scared or don't know how to proceed. But just because she's so damn beautiful.

"Thank you," I whisper.

Jackie nods and then wraps me in a hug.

NINE

I INHALE the scent of Jackie's hair, her perfume. I bury my face in her neck, wanting to stay here. Jackie pulls away, almost instinctively. Like she wants nothing to happen and I clear my throat.

"Thank you," I repeat, though this time it's more formal.

"Of course," Jackie says. "I should probably head out," she adds.

I nod and walk her to the door.

"Call me if you need anything. Anything at all," she says.

Her eyes linger on mine a moment longer than necessary. The two of us stand there silently, taking each other in. I want to tell her to stay. That I need her right now. But I don't. I just smile and nod before I close the door.

I lean against it and slide to the floor, the sticky note still in my hand.

I rest my forearms on my knees and look at the note again.

Owe Blankenships $155,000 by Friday

Could this have been about something else? Maybe a different Friday that he'd owed them some money. Likely, he made good on it. It was probably just a reminder, phrased in a certain way that would make it clear to Billy what he needed to take care of.

That's all it was.

Wasn't it?

Jackie worked with Billy. She saw him every day. If anyone would know anything suspicious about what was going on at his office, it would be her. Absolutely one-hundred percent her. And I trust Jackie. She's had my back more times than I can really count.

I count on her to have it this time for certain.

I think about the bruising on Billy's face when I saw him in the pool. Could that have been from an encounter with Dan, wanting his money? Could Billy not have gotten it to them on time?

But why would they kill him over that? Why wouldn't they want him alive so he could get the money if he didn't have it?

But he did have it. He employed Jackie. We had this house to show for it. Olivia's schooling. The cars. Everything.

I've never had to worry about money the whole time I've been with Billy. The security is something that attracted me to him. Not the idea that I'd be marrying rich, but the idea that I'd never have to worry. It was stability. It was Olivia's future. It was freedom of choice.

Billy had provided us with all of that.

I look at the note once again.

I think about seeing Amanda buying the burner phones at the super center.

The only reason that they'd want those phones is so that they could talk to each other and not leave much of a trail. I'd seen enough true crime shows to know that.

Immediately, I stand up from my seat on the floor and I rush over to the counter where my purse is. I fish out my phone and lean against the counter on my elbows. I go to social media and I look Amanda up.

I scroll through her feed. Pictures of her and Dan at sporting events, sitting in the best seats. Pictures of them on cruises, always in a suite. Pictures of luxury vacations in distant places that most people only dream of. They are the quintessential power couple that has chosen career and freedom over having kids.

They're enviable. Even to me.

I would never trade Olivia for anything, but I can see how this lifestyle could be amazing.

I scroll on.

Amanda has shared various charities, asking for donations for this or that. The stuff that mainly rich people donate to. Medical research foundations. The arts and the library. All of the fundraisers have involved galas and balls and dinners. The kind of stuff your run-of-the-mill family doesn't really attend. This is for the super rich in the area.

Dallas's elite.

Those are the circles they run in. Which makes me wonder why they ever thought they should be friends with us. Maybe it was out of necessity. It's hard when you live a different lifestyle than most people. Hard to find other people that think similarly, even harder still to find ones you like. And Dan and Amanda seemed to like us.

Maybe that's all it was. We all lived the same way.

They felt understood, probably in a way that they didn't with their hoity-toity charity ball friends.

I think about the burner phones and the note that Jackie shared with me. It all seems to add up quickly, stacking evidence that's not in their favor.

I keep looking.

There's a picture of Dan and Amanda at one of these charity events and in the background I see a familiar face that I had no idea attended such things.

Billy.

I feel a stabbing sensation in my chest. Almost like an actual knife being thrust into me. Why would he be here and not tell me about it?

In the background, he's laughing with someone just off camera. A woman? I wonder. Why would he keep this a secret otherwise?

My face goes hot and my stomach sour.

Could Billy have been having an affair? Could I have missed that?

I always think it's strange when women say they had no idea that their husband was cheating on them. I think you would know. You could sense it. Feel it. Something would be off between the two of you. Something would be off about his behavior. I swear that if that was the case, I would have suspected something.

But then I think about Billy managing money for our friends and not even telling me about it.

Maybe I didn't know him as well as I thought I did.

I stare at the picture, trying to imagine what he was saying to whoever is just off camera. The mystery person who's just to the right. I wonder who they are. Why they were there? I wonder if they left together?

I know I was ready for my marriage to Billy to be over, but this is a betrayal, anyway.

Maybe it was his way of punishing me. He always thought that my desire to be non-monogamous meant that I was a cheater. I tried to explain to him that it's different. It's only cheating when the other person doesn't know about it and wouldn't be okay with it. Maybe it had gotten to where it really was cheating after Billy stopped taking part. Maybe this was his way of getting back at me. His way of punishing me for being a terrible wife.

Maybe I deserved it.

Maybe I really wasn't a good wife.

Maybe I'd never been cut out to be a wife.

Much less a mother.

I lock my phone and place it on the counter, a million things swirling around in my head. It's like someone had gone into the dusty attic of my mind and stomped around, stirring up all the dust and dirt. Stuff that I wasn't really ready to deal with right now.

I think about everything that's happened in the last eighteen to twenty-four hours. My husband is dead. Jackie thinks our friends had something to do with it, and it's certainly looking like that could be the case. A detective obviously suspects me. My daughter is in shock. Everything is very, very wrong.

I open my phone back up and the screen is still

showing that picture of Dan and Amanda with Billy in the background.

My eyes trace his features. His always perfect brown hair, his gleaming smile. In his hand, he has a drink. Whiskey, most likely. That was always his alcohol of choice.

I wonder what I was doing when this picture was taken. I wonder if it was one night that he'd told me he was working late. Had I been stupid to believe him? To just take that at face value?

I don't want to think that I was.

But I feel like I'm seeing things clearly for the first time amid all of this.

I'm realizing that there's a very distinct possibility that I never knew my husband at all.

TEN

MY PHONE RINGS.

Before I can get caught up in the train of thought I'm trying to pursue, I have to answer it. When I look at the number, it's one I don't recognize, but it's local. This ties my gut in a knot, making me want to vomit.

There's really only one person it might be.

"Hello," I say. A statement, not a meek greeting.

"Mrs. Karlsen, this is Troy," Detective Underwood says on the other end of the line.

"I thought it might be you," I say.

"Oh?" He pauses, leaving room for me to respond, but I don't. If I hadn't realized we were in a game of cat and mouse, I would in this moment. Underwood suspects me. He goes on when I don't bite. "I wondered if I'd be able to see you today to ask you some more questions."

"Don't I need to come down to the station for something like that?" I ask, annoyance dripping off each word. I'm sleep deprived and have an emotional hangover from everything happening in my life.

"Oh, nothing so formal," he says, and I hear a smile in his voice.

Suddenly, he reminds me of all the guys that my mom dated after my dad left. Slimy, looking for an opportunity, and total predators.

She didn't have to associate with those assholes.

But in this case, I do.

"Well, what then?" I ask. My words are clipped.

"I was wondering if I'd be able to come see you at your house," Underwood says. "Just have a little chat with you."

"That's fine."

I'm not sure that it is. I feel a little like I might need a lawyer. A lawyer would make me look guilty, wouldn't they? I think of all the true crime shows where I've urged the person to get a lawyer, knowing they were innocent. But now, in the middle of it, it's an actual dilemma. I think about the news coverage. How would it look? Would it hurt me if I went to trial for Billy's murder? I don't know. A million things are racing through my mind.

"What time works for you?" Underwood asks.

His tone is calm, easygoing, almost like he's making plans for brunch with an old friend. It's almost disarming. It might be if I didn't have my guard up so high.

I wonder if it's worked for him before on other people.

My guess is yes.

"Right now," I say, figuring that I'm playing chess with this guy. What better time to suggest than right this second? That's what an innocent person would do, right?

What the hell am I thinking? I am an innocent person.

My thoughts are absurd. I take a breath.

"Great," Underwood says.

He doesn't debate the time. That makes me wonder if there really ever was a choice. If right now is what he would have suggested all along.

Touche, Troy.

"I'll see you soon," he says.

And then he hangs up the phone.

I'm left holding mine, wondering if he has any actual evidence against me. I go back over the scene, the evening, trying to identify anything suspicious about it or my behavior.

I can't come up with anything.

But that doesn't mean Troy hasn't.

I TELL Olivia to stay in her room for a while. She gives me a funny look.

"Why?"

"Someone is coming to talk to me about what happened to your step-dad last night," I tell her, not wanting to mention that the someone is actually a detective.

Olivia just shrugs and powers on her Xbox.

I close the door and breathe a sigh of relief. I don't know what I had planned to say if she had a lot of questions about who was coming. As far as Olivia knows, it was an accident, plain and simple. Or at least, I'm assuming that's what she thinks. I haven't really taken the time to give her any explanation.

I need to do that.

God. The list of things I need to take care of seems to climb astronomically taller by the minute. I head into the kitchen and for a moment; I think about having a drink. Something strong. I decide against it, knowing that it would only give Underwood more ammunition against me. Something that he would feel painted me as guilty. The woman who couldn't give an interview to a detective about her husband's death without being drunk.

That's a headline.

I sit down in the living room and flip on the television while I wait for Underwood, not that I'm going to concentrate on anything. I change the channel from daytime talk shows to the noon news. And what the anchor is saying stops me, my blood running cold and sending a chill throughout my body.

"We have some breaking news: last night, a rising star financial advisor, William Karlsen, was found dead in his pool. There is an ongoing investigation into what happened to Mr. Karlsen. It's unknown who will take over his firm for his clients."

Next to the brunette anchor is a picture of Billy.

And next to him is me. Smiling.

It was from our honeymoon. They must have pulled it from social media.

Somehow, it feels like a violation. Like they've overstepped their bounds. I know Billy was well known in the

Dallas social circles. Elite members of the community made up his clientele. I didn't expect his death to make the news, though.

The thought is horrifying.

I wonder how many people that knew him saw it just now. I wonder if they're going to keep covering the story.

I feel sick when there's a knock at the door. I switch off the TV and stand, wiping my sweaty palms on my jeans. I go open the door and give Detective Underwood a demure smile.

"Come in," I say, doing my best impression of a grieving widow.

I am grieving; I remind myself. Maybe it doesn't look like the usual grief you see. There aren't any tears, but there are a lot of hard feelings.

There's a lot I'd still like to say to Billy. A lot of things I'd like for him to know at this point. Things I wasn't ready to really commit to saying yet when he was alive. Now that he's dead, it seems almost unfair. I never got to leave him.

Correction: I never made the choice to leave him.

That might be what hurts most of all. I just stayed. Something I swore I would never do.

"Good afternoon, Mrs. Karlsen," Underwood says as he comes inside the house. He looks around, like he's seeing it for the first time all over again.

"Same as it was last night," I say with a tight smile.

"It's a lovely place you've got here," he says. "You two must do well for yourselves," he adds and glances at me, his gaze heavy.

Underwood has the kind of eyes that people talk about seeing right through you. Not because they're piercing blue, but because there's something behind the expression. An intelligence that lets you know nothing gets by him.

If I were a criminal, I'd find it unnerving.

Once again, I have to remind myself I'm not one.

"We do," I say. "Thanks."

"Billy had a big financial firm I understand," Underwood goes on.

"That's correct," I say.

"So, he managed money for a lot of people," he adds, looking around the living room, examining items in the bookcases. "Did he ever mismanage anyone's money?" he asks.

"Not that I'm aware of," I say.

Then I think of the note that Jackie brought me. The one that made it seem like he'd owed quite a bit of money to Dan and Amanda.

Is that enough for me to bring it to his attention?

No, it's absurd. Jackie's wrong.

But it was one of you.

A little voice reminds me of this. That one or more of the seven of us had something to do with this.

Why couldn't it be them?

I'm about to bring it up when Underwood moves on.

"Did your husband have any strained relationships?" he asks.

"Everyone liked Billy," I say. It's true. Everyone liked him. He had that charisma outside of the house. And apparently with Olivia. I guess he only took the mask off for me. How lucky.

"Including you," Underwood says, looking over at me. His eyes linger, gauging my reaction.

"Including me," I say.

"You had a solid marriage?" he probes.

"We fought like any married couple," I say. "We had our problems."

"Any big problems? Ones you didn't think you could solve?"

He reminds me of a wolf again. And the more he does, the more I feel like a wounded deer, sensing that a predator is tailing me.

"None that I would have murdered him over," I say with a bitter laugh.

"You don't seem very distraught over his death," Underwood remarks.

"Is that a crime, Detective?" I ask.

"Not at all," he says. "But it's unusual."

He picks up something from the bookshelf. A jar of sand that Billy and I gathered on our honeymoon. The same honeymoon where we took the picture that was just on the news.

"It's from our honeymoon," I tell him without thinking.

"My wife and I have one, too," he says. "Ex-wife, I should say."

"Divorced?" I ask.

"Headed that way," he admits.

"I'm sorry about that," I say.

"Don't be. It's not your fault," he says with a smile as he puts the sand back.

I say nothing else.

"Look, Mrs. Karlsen," Underwood says, placing his hands in the pockets of his brown suit. "If there's anything that you need to tell me, you need to tell me now. Not later."

"I didn't kill my husband, if that's what you're getting at," I say.

He shrugs his shoulders.

"It's your choice," he says.

I scoff.

"Are you telling me you think I killed Billy?" I ask.

"I've worked a lot of homicides and you wouldn't believe how many times it turns out that the spouse did it."

"So you're just going to apply that percentage to this case and not actually work it?" I ask.

An expression of annoyance flits over his features. I've bothered him.

"Not at all," Underwood says. "I intend to turn every stone. I'm just saying if you know of something hiding under one of them, it would be to your benefit to tell me now about what I'm going to find."

"Oh, because you're on my side?" I snap, realizing almost instantly I shouldn't have.

His eyes narrow. He's losing patience.

"I'm not on anyone's side here except for the deceased," he says.

I cross my arms over my chest.

"Are we done?" I ask, grabbing the doorknob.

"I suppose so," Underwood says.

"Then leave."

"Oh, one last thing, Mrs. Karlsen. I've got a warrant that we'll need to be executing to search your home and your husband's office," he adds. "See you soon."

ELEVEN

I'M SEETHING as I slam the door after Underwood.

I rub my temples and pace, feeling the weight of what just happened cascade over me. He really suspects me. He's zeroed in on me.

The thought makes my heart flutter with panic. It almost feels the same as young love. Both of them indicating danger ahead.

"What was that?" Olivia asks.

I snap my head up and see her standing in the hallway, holding her Xbox controller, her headset hanging around her neck.

"Nothing, honey," I say.

"Was that a detective?" she asks.

I've made it a point not to lie to Olivia as much as I can. Even when she was tiny, I tried to be as truthful as I could with her at an appropriate level for her age.

I hesitate.

"Mom, what happened last night?" she asks.

Her tone is serious.

"We found your step-dad in the pool," I say. "Jackie and I did. We couldn't get him to breathe. The person who was just here is just trying to find out if this was an accident," I say.

"So, it was a detective," she says, her tone accusatory.

"Yes," I say.

Olivia's jaw sets and I see tears in her eyes. She stares at me and I see the judgment on her face. I can see what she's thinking. She's misplacing blame. A coping mechanism. But part of me wonders if it's really all that misplaced.

Then she turns and goes back to her bedroom, slamming the door behind herself. I cringe at the sound, feeling like I've failed her in so many ways. I wish that I could protect her from this. I think about what it will be like for her to go back to school.

Not only will she be the girl whose step-dad was on the news, found dead in his pool. She'll be the one whose mom is being investigated for the death.

The thought makes me sick.

And I'm sure it's something that has occurred to Olivia. She's a smart kid. And teenagers can be cruel.

I think about going to her room, trying to talk to her. I hesitate.

God, I wish Michael were here.

Michael was always the one that was good at this part.

Maybe I'm emotionally unavailable, just like my mom was with me. I've always sworn I'd never end up like her. And now, I think I have. It's impossible to talk to my daughter about how she's feeling. Her father is so much better at that than me. She meets his input with a grateful smile and she just glares at me any time I try.

I grab my phone and dial Michael's number.

"What's going on?" Michael asks instead of hello.

"The whole world is going to shit," I tell him with a bitter laugh.

"You guys okay?" I can almost hear him sitting up straighter and rolling out of bed.

"We're fine," I assure him. "I just—the detective working Billy's death was just here."

"And?" Michael asks.

"It didn't go very well," I tell him. "I think he suspects me of having something to do with it."

"Jesus Christ," Michael says with a sigh. "How's Liv?"

"Mad at me," I say. "She's in her room right now. I think she blames me for the whole thing."

"Are you sure you guys are okay?" Michael asks. "Do you want me to come over?"

"No, no," I say. "Not necessary."

"You wouldn't have called me if you didn't want someone to tell you everything's alright," Michael says, cutting through my bullshit. He has a way of that.

I chuckle.

"I guess you're right," I say. "But I refuse to make you come over."

"We live one neighborhood apart, Kim," Michael says.

It's true. We stayed close together for Olivia's sake, even though Billy thought it might be a good idea to put some space between me and my ex-husband. Eventually, Olivia's best interest won out.

"Still, just talk to me," I say.

The way I say it reminds me of back when Michael and I were dating. How we'd stay up all night on the phone, even when both of us had to work or go to school the next morning. We were high school sweethearts and had Olivia young. I dropped out of high school and got my GED. Michael went to college. Became an engineer.

"Okay," he breathes. I wonder if it's reminding him of the same thing. "Everything's going to be alright, Kim," he says. "You're just on his radar right now. He'll give up as soon as he clears you," Michael goes on. "I imagine he's seen a lot of wives kill their rich husbands," he adds with a chuckle.

I don't reply right away. All I can think about is that I was one of three people to find him dead. It doesn't really bode well for being cleared. I sigh.

"I hope you're right," I say.

"What do you think happened?" Michael asks.

"I don't know, honestly," I say.

"Who else was there?"

"Jason, Nicole, Dan and Amanda, Nathan, Jackie, and me," I say.

"Right, a party," he says.

"Right," I whisper.

"That complicates it, doesn't it?" he asks.

I sigh, glad he's not trying to make me feel worse.

"It does," I say. "We're our alibis. And everyone had to lie," I say.

"Shit," Michael says.

"Tell me about it," I say.

"Who do you think it could have been?" he asks.

"I don't know," I say. But immediately, the note that Jackie gave me comes to mind. "Well, I may have some idea," I tell him.

"Who?"

"So, apparently Billy owed some money to Dan and Amanda," I say.

"What? How'd you find that out?" he asks.

"Jackie showed me a note she found on Billy's desk," I say.

"Shit," Michael says. Then he's silent for a moment.

We stay on the phone, hashing out the details, working through everyone who was at the party and returning to the Blankenships. Michael urges me to tell Detective Underwood.

"Just based on a sticky note?" I ask him.

"It's the best piece of evidence you've got right now. Besides, wouldn't it be nice for him to get off your back?" he asks.

"Actually, I may have one other piece of evidence."

"What?"

"I saw Amanda buying burner phones this morning," I tell him.

"Wait, what?" Michael asks.

"I saw her at the super center and she was putting two pre-paid phones into her basket, Michael," I say.

He's silent for a moment.

"Yeah, you need to tell the detective about that, Kim," he says.

I want to just agree with him. Like it's that easy. But I'm not sure that it is.

I care about these people. But my husband was just murdered.

It's more complicated than outsiders might think it is.

But I know it's the right thing to do. Michael's absolutely right.

I need to talk to Underwood. And I need to cooperate with him if I want to stay out of jail.

TWELVE

I MULL ALL of this over for the rest of the afternoon.

I need to make a call to Underwood, but I'm hesitating. Maybe it's just extreme empathy making me not want to tell him the truth. I don't know why—other than owing them money—they would want Billy dead. It still doesn't make sense. If he's dead, how are they going to get their money back?

Something about it doesn't add up.

But it's the best I've got.

At around five, Olivia emerges from her bedroom like a gremlin coming out to graze before going back to its nest for the winter.

I'm sitting at the bar when she goes through the refrigerator.

She pulls out the salad that she got earlier.

"I want mine, too," I tell her.

She gets it and grabs me a fork, silently putting both of them in front of me.

She opens her salad and eats.

Tension permeates the air. I can feel her judgment. I hate it even though I know I deserve it.

But then she speaks.

"It's not your fault, Mom," she says.

I almost choke on the greens I'm swallowing.

I look into her eyes and see the pain there. Even as I do, I know that there's always this invisible wall between us and that she and her dad exist on one side of it, and I exist on the other. Just for a moment, I'd like to be on their side.

It physically pains me.

"You don't have to tell me that, Liv," I say.

"No, I mean it," she says, sounding wise beyond her years. "It's just a terrible situation."

I raise an eyebrow, a little surprised by her maturity.

"That it is," I agree.

I forbid myself from saying more, putting any of it on her. She eats her salad quietly. Finally, I broach the silence this time.

"Would you like to make some cookies?"

She looks at me and her features perk up, reminding me of a dog that just heard the word outside. It makes me smile a little.

"I'd like that," she says, smiling back at me.

We finish our salads, making small talk, both of us attempting something close to a mother-daughter bond. Something that I've always felt was just out of my reach, but in this moment, it feels close.

It feels like it's something we could actually have.

I get the ingredients out to make cookies and Olivia helps me.

It reminds me of a show I used to watch. When one character's boyfriend died, she went into a baking frenzy, making muffins for days. More than anyone in her household could eat before they went bad. Suddenly, I feel like this is the perfect way to deal with a death. At least as long as it means Olivia is standing next to me.

I want to keep outrunning reality for her.

We scoop the chocolate chip dough out into little balls and place them on a baking sheet and throw the first batch into the oven. Olivia grabs a Dr. Pepper from the fridge and takes a seat at the bar, pulling out her phone to text her friends or scroll on her favorite app.

I'm content now. I grab some wine and pour a glass and I lean against the counter, just soaking up the moment.

I wish we could stay here. That we didn't have to go back to the real world on Monday.

I look up at Olivia.

"Hey," I say.

She looks up from her phone.

"What if you don't go back to school yet?" I ask.

Her eyes light up, like any kid's, at the prospect of not having to go to school on Monday morning. I smile despite myself.

"Yes, please," Olivia says, sounding almost desperate.

The moment shifts, going from one of amusement to something darker. I realize in her expression that she knows what's waiting for her back at school. It makes a stone drop in my gut, reminding me of exactly what's going on in our lives.

I force a smile at her.

"You got it, kiddo."

WE ENJOY the cookies less than I thought we would.

We're back to reality now. Olivia disappears into her room and I'm left on the couch, avoiding the news like it's Ebola. The last thing I want is to be surprised by Billy's face on my screen. It feels like a nightmare from which I'll never emerge.

The thought is daunting.

I remind myself of what Michael said. I need to call Underwood. I need to tell him what I know. Even if it's nothing.

Nothing will ever be the same between any of us, I realize.

One of them killed your husband, Kim.

A low voice whispers through my mind. Treacherous. Dangerous.

And I wrestle with the thought that I might be grateful to whichever of them did so.

I can't help them get away with a crime just because Billy was a piece of shit.

Can I?

Just as I ponder this question, my phone rings and startles me out of my deep philosophical rabbit hole.

The same number as earlier.

It's Underwood.

"Can I help you?" I ask when I pick up the phone, unable to stop myself.

"Mrs. Karlsen, this is—"

"Yeah, I know it's you," I say.

"I was just calling to let you know that your husband's remains have been released for funeral arrangements. You just need to call your funeral home of choice and have them pick him up from the ME's office," he says.

"Somehow, I doubt this is the only reason you're calling me," I say.

"I thought you'd be grateful for that," he says, his southern accent melodic yet threatening.

"Why did you really call?"

"I also wanted to tell you I'd love to discuss the autopsy results with you," he says. Then he adds, "they got to your husband quickly at my request." And then he pauses.

"Well?" I prompt him.

"Oh, it can wait until after the funeral," Detective Underwood says. And there's the hint of amusement in his voice. Something wolfish, too. Like he knows he's got something he can hold over me. It makes my skin crawl.

"Fine," I say, hoping my irritation doesn't show.

If he wants to play a game of cat and mouse, he's in over his head. I learned from the best. A bitter detective is no match for a girl that grew up with a lioness stalking the hallways of her childhood home. My mother was simply the best player in that game to exist.

I spent all of my youth playing games with my mother, learning it was never safe to show my emotions because she might use them against me. It's probably the reason I am the way I am with Olivia. Not that I think she'd do the same.

It's part of me, like freckles on my skin.

Telling him to fuck off is tempting, but I know that's not an option. I've been pretty hostile, but that would be pushing it, making him suspect me more than he already does. I sigh.

"What's wrong, Mrs. Karlsen?" he asks.

"Nothing," I say with false pleasantness. I don't want him to see me sweat, even though my palms are clammy and I can feel a dampness under my arms. He's getting to me.

"I'll see you after the funeral," he says before hanging up.

I stare at the phone for a moment, scared of what news it might bring next. I cradle it in my palm, not moving, almost like it's a sleeping pit viper and I'm trying not to upset it.

I shake the image off and send a text message to Michael.

Hey.

It's only a moment before he texts me back.

What's up?

That's one of the many things I can count on Michael for. Quick text responses.

They're releasing Billy's body. Can you go to the funeral home with me tomorrow morning?

It's a weird ask. And I wouldn't blame Michael a bit if he didn't want to go. How weird is this situation? Burying your dead husband and making all the arrangements with your ex at your side? Not great optics, I think.

But Michael is the person I go to when I need comfort. He's the person who's always there for me, even after the dissolution of our marriage. Michael is a good friend.

Of course.

He doesn't even hesitate to answer.

It's then that I feel a hot tear snake down my cheek. An admission from my body, a betrayal.

I am stressed. This is stressful. Underwood's call is getting under my skin.

And I'm scared.

Just putting the thought into words inside my mind is terrifying. It makes the fear real. It makes real the consequences that I might face for something I didn't even do.

I need to tell Underwood about Dan and Amanda, the burner phones, and the note that Jackie found on Billy's desk.

There's no doubt about it. My freedom may depend on the information I have.

And for Christ's sake, they might have murdered Billy.

I thank Michael and I switch over to the thread I share with Jackie. I send her a quick message, asking her if she can watch Olivia in the morning. She responds after a few minutes.

Of course!!!

Her enthusiasm in text is true to how she is in real life. She hates for anyone not to feel included or important or worthy of getting excited about. Maybe this is a weird instance to show it, but it's her way of being there for me. And watching Olivia helps.

I stare at my phone for a moment.

I get on the search engine and look for funeral homes

near me. I find one that has five stars on their reviews. I dial the number.

"Pickard and Sons Funeral Home, this is Amy. How can I help you?" a young woman with a soft voice asks from the other end of the line. Her presence is instantly soothing and I think she's gone into the right line of work.

"I need to make arrangements for my husband. He's at the ME's office right now," I say.

"Alright, let me take down your information," she says.

We go through the back and forth of her getting his name, my name, a phone number, setting up a time for me to meet with the funeral director in the morning. 10:00 sharp. I thank her and we get off the phone. I text Michael the time and update Jackie on when she needs to pick Olivia up.

Then I sit there, staring into nothingness.

I don't feel numb anymore.

Underwood's voice echoes through my mind.

I feel scared.

And I never feel scared.

THIRTEEN

TWO THINGS HAPPEN the next morning. The search and the funeral arrangements. Underwood and his cops show up early and they ransack the place. They copy everything from the computer and make a mess behind themselves.

The cops don't take long, but they're thorough, focusing on Billy's office. In the middle of it all, I ask Jackie to come get Olivia and keep her for the rest of the day.

She takes Olivia to get ice cream, getting her out of the way. About ten minutes after they leave, I heard the rumble of Michael's truck in the driveway.

Michael stays with me as the cops wrap up and we watch as they leave to head to Billy's office.

The rumble of the truck brings a memory, sharp as the cut-off lid of an aluminum can. *Billy*. When he would hear Michael's truck in the driveway. Billy would always say, "There's your ex-husband and his substitute for masculinity."

I always bit down on the urge to tell him that when it came to manhood, Michael had him beat in every arena. Especially the one where it came to being nice to your spouse. But I never did.

Holding back was so unlike me.

When I'd been with Michael, I'd never had a problem telling him how it was or what I did or didn't like that he did. He did the same with me. But unlike Billy, he never belittled me in the process or denigrated my choices.

It seemed like Billy excelled at that.

I breathe a sigh of relief because I don't have to hear his bullshit today. He's dead.

I grab my purse and head out to the truck. Michael rolls down the window and whistles at me playfully.

"Shut up," I say, not really in the mood.

Michael holds up a hand in apology and I get into the passenger side of the truck.

"Sorry, just wanted to make you laugh," he says.

"I'm sorry," I apologize, too. "I'm just on edge."

"Did you tell that detective the stuff you told me?" Michael asks.

I know he means well, but it feels like pressure. It feels like he's going to be disappointed in me when I tell him I haven't.

"Not yet," I say, hedging it.

"You really need to, Kim," he says.

"Since when do I let you tell me what to do?" I ask, smirking at him, trying to be playful. Trying not to let my mask slip and let him see exactly how freaked out I am about the whole thing.

He's right, though.

We drive in silence the rest of the way to the funeral home. I don't really know what to say. Michael and I have never struggled for words, but today we seem at a loss. Like both of us are afraid of what might come out of our mouths.

Sometimes I miss Michael, and having him with me today is a blessing.

"Thank you for taking me," I say, venturing to break the silence first.

"Of course," he says, glancing over at me briefly. "You've always been there for me, Kim. Least I can do is return the favor."

I know there's more to it than that, though.

If I told Michael to jump, he'd ask, "How high?"

I know he would. He's been there for me more solidly than any human being I've ever known. I love Michael, even if I'm not in love with him anymore.

My eyes linger on him after he turns back to face the steering wheel. I think about all the times we had together. The good ones especially. Maybe it's the nature of the day, but I want to look at my past with him through rose-colored glasses. Maybe it's just easy to do that when contrasting it with how Billy treated me.

I was never fully honest with Michael about any of that. I knew he'd be horrified.

We pull into the lot of the funeral home and I see the huge black and white sign that declares this to be Pickard and Sons Funeral Home. Right beside it is a cemetery. I look out over the gravestones as Michael parks, wondering what the story is for each of those people buried out there. I unbuckle my seatbelt and don't break my gaze.

I wonder if any of them were murdered.

I wondered if any of their murders were solved.

The thought sends a chill down my arms. I want to tell Michael to back out. To go pick up Olivia and hit the highway, take us somewhere far away from this. But it's all fantasy.

I know what I'm facing when I walk through those doors.

Reality.

The last funeral I planned was my mother's, and that was rife with just as many mixed emotions as this one will be.

"Well, we're here," Michael says about twenty seconds after he kills the engine. I'm still sitting there staring out over the cemetery, wondering about the people buried here.

"We're here," I say, turning back to face him. I offer a small smile. I feel small. Like a version of myself that's been swallowed up nine times over.

I hate it.

We get out of the truck and Michael holds the door for me when we walk in. I step inside and spot a young woman at a desk near the front door. She's on the phone.

"We'll see you then," she says. "Thank you."

And then she hangs up, turning her attention to us.

"You must be Mrs. Karlsen," she says and stands. She sticks out a hand to shake mine.

Then she reaches her hand out for Michael's.

He shakes and nods without saying anything.

She looks at him for a moment, and I can see the mental calculation going on. She's trying to figure out who he is to me. If he's a brother, a cousin. Surely not a lover.

I want to tell her he's none of those things. Just a friend. But it seems like that would only make things more awkward.

"Right this way," she says after grabbing a folder.

She leads us down a narrow hallway off the main lobby area. The whole place is furnished lavishly. It reminds me of old money. Dark woods and lush upholstery. The kind of furnishings and decor that you'd find in an older person's house who had hired a decorator for a large sum of money. I wonder if they did it themselves. If that's intentional.

She shows us to a room that has a long oval table in it. There are three seats on either side. At the head of the table is a china cabinet that displays a horde of treasures.

"Derek will be right with you," Amy says. And then she pulls the door almost closed and heads back down the hallway.

I step over to the head of the table and start examining everything in the cabinet.

Urns and jewelry made for storing ashes. Laser engraved images of your loved ones. Thumbprint necklaces. Angel figurines with specific dates painted at their base. They have something for everyone.

It's strange how commercialized this business has become.

I don't remember these things being available when I buried my mom. But maybe that was because I took her to the cheapest place we could find. At eighteen, I didn't have any money to give her a good send off. And I'm not sure I would have even if I'd had the money for it.

Part of me feels the same about Billy. Maybe we should have just gone somewhere cheap that would have put him in a rental casket, let his friends look at him for a couple of days, and then pulled the bottom out and slid him right into the crematory.

The thought doesn't even make me flinch. It would have been closer to what he deserved.

"Funeral homes are always strange, aren't they?" Michael asks.

"Indeed," I say, standing up from my bent over position.

I take a seat at the table. Michael's looking at another display and picks something up.

"Can you imagine keeping one of these in your house?" he asks while turning around with a very breakable looking urn.

"A lot of people do," I tell him, but his expression makes me laugh.

He shudders.

"I'd just as soon any dead bodies go underground where they belong."

He puts it back.

"Sit down and quit judging the way other people grieve," I tell him.

He comes around the table and takes a seat next to me. He reaches for my hand and squeezes it.

"I'm glad you asked me to come with you today," he says.

"Why? So you could get an up close and personal tour of Pickard and Sons?" I ask.

He stares at me, and I have to look away. There's something about it, his gaze, that makes me shift in my seat. I look back up at him.

"Michael," I say.

"I'm just glad to be with you," he whispers.

Just then, the door creaks open and in comes a portly man in a suit with a clipboard and a pen.

"You must be Mrs. Karlsen," he says to me, sticking out his hand.

I have to let go of Michael's hand to stand up and shake this man's.

He glances at Michael and then turns to face him.

"Derek," he says.

"Michael."

"Have a seat, folks," Derek says.

He gathers the papers in the folder that Amy came in here with, but several times he looks over at Michael, clearly doing the same thing that Amy was. Trying to work out what sort of relationship we have. Who he is to me.

"Michael's my ex-husband," I blurt out, sick of it.

Derek looks at me, eyes wide.

"Oh, I—uhh," he stammers.

"It's okay," I say. "Let's just get on with it."

And then Derek buries his nose in the folder, trying to find the first piece of paper he needs.

I SLIDE my giant shades onto my face as we emerge into the blistering July sunshine. It's approaching noon, and the heat is out in full force. It wouldn't surprise me if I cracked an egg on one of the rocks in the flowerbed and it cooked instantly.

I could take a swim when I get home.

No.

The thought turns my stomach. The idea of being in the same water Billy drowned in. It feels like his death might be infectious, traveling in molecules spread throughout the pool, waiting to claim someone else.

The thought is absurd, but I realize instantly that I don't want Olivia swimming in there. At least for now.

It makes me think about the way we touch the dead. Or avoid touching them, I guess. Like we think we can be contaminated. That some great grim reaper will stir at the sensation of our fingertips brushing across their cold, clammy hand.

I can remember touching my mother. She lay there in the casket, so still that I could swear I saw her breathing. Her face was made up in a way that she never would have approved of. Her blush too bright and high on her cheeks, her lips an awful dusty rose. She usually wore a deep red. And I'll never forget when the funeral director came in to put in her earrings.

I sat there as he shoved the post through, her flesh giving and making the most awful popping noise. He smiled at me and left, like this was normal. Like everyone should be familiar with the sound of steel rammed through a dead person's earlobes.

I'm glad, suddenly, that Billy didn't have pierced ears. You never would have caught him dead with jewelry on.

For marrying a woman that didn't want to be monogamous, Billy had a lot of conservative views on things. Like whether men should wear jewelry. And whether women should be in love with other women.

He never wanted me to be alone with Jackie. That was something we'd agreed on. I wasn't supposed to entertain anyone without him knowing about it. It was sort of an unspoken rule in the group as well. Swinging was different from cheating. Cheating implied that it was going on behind someone's back. As long as you were honest with each other, it was one thing. But when you started sneaking around, having feelings, that was an entirely other thing.

A crow caws across the cemetery and I'm brought back to reality.

"You alright?" Michael asks me.

"I'm fine," I tell him with a smile that feels a little forced.

How fine am I supposed to be? I just made arrangements to bury my husband who died Friday night. A detective clearly thinks I had something to do with it. And I'm here with my ex-husband while my teenage daughter will barely look at me because she blames me for the whole thing.

I think women have to do this a lot. Be fine when they're not.

"I'm fine," I repeat, but mostly for my benefit and not for Michael's.

His gaze lingers on me before he puts on his

RayBans. I can tell he senses I'm not fine, but he knows that pushing me rarely ends well for him. I'll likely snap at him like I did the other day. I'm grateful to him for not bringing it up, although I owe him an apology.

The crow caws again, and I look for it. But my eyes find something else across the cemetery, parked near a monument replica of the pieta.

A black sedan with windows so dark you could never guess who was inside of it.

My stomach drops, like I'm plummeting over the first hill of a roller coaster.

I stand there, motionless, like this is a dinosaur movie and if I'm still enough, whoever is in the car won't see me.

"You ready?" Michael asks.

I startle, nearly jumping back into the flowerbed and landing on the skillet-hot rocks inside it.

"Yeah," I say. I look back at the sedan, and it's just sitting there. I wonder if whoever is inside is watching us. If they followed us here. "Let's go," I say.

I take my attention off the car and climb into Michael's truck. I pull down the passenger side visor and look into the mirror, acting like I'm checking my makeup when I'm really keeping an eye on the sedan behind us. It's probably a football field away. It'll take a little time for the car to catch up to us once we turn onto Main Street.

Won't it?

You're being ridiculous.

I tell myself this, like my thought about the contaminated pool, is absurd.

Lots of people drive black sedans. And lots of them

have major tinting on the windows. That's nothing to write home about.

But when we back out of the parking space, I see the sedan move, heading for the exit to the cemetery, which emerges onto the street right next to the one leading out of the funeral home parking lot.

Michael pulls us to the entrance and my heart races.

I sit there silently, not wanting to bring it up with him because the chance that it's really even the same person, and that they're following me, is ludicrous.

Still, I stare into the rearview, my mouth growing cottony dry as the car approaches the exit next to us.

"Go," I tell Michael instinctively.

He glances at me, wondering what the hell I'm talking about.

"Go!" I insist.

He whips out into traffic and a car nearly rear ends us. But there's a stream of other cars from the light not far behind. The black sedan is going to have a hard time getting out. If we can make it to the next light just before it turns red, we might be out of their reach.

"What's wrong?" Michael asks.

He glances in the rearview mirror.

"That guy nearly hit us," he says.

I say nothing, scanning the mirror for any sign of the black sedan.

I don't see it.

"Nothing's wrong," I say. "I'm just ready to be home."

I smile at Michael, but he eyes me in a way that makes me think he doesn't believe me at all.

FOURTEEN

"YOU WANT SOME ICE CREAM?" Michael asks me after we buckle ourselves in.

"Sure, why not?" I say.

Today couldn't get weirder. Being at the funeral home with my ex-husband, having just planned my dead husband's funeral, and thought someone was following us. Why shouldn't we go for an ice cream date before going back to the house? Jackie had nowhere to be today. She won't mind if we take our time.

Jackie.

The thought of her stirs up the memory of her scent. And then I think about the taste of her kiss on Friday night.

I physically shake my head, silently telling myself there is nothing more inappropriate that I could think about right now, minutes after making the final arrangements for the man we found dead in my pool only moments after that kiss.

I'm sick.

I feel like I need someone to hose me down or pour ice water over my head. I push the memory away, deep down, into the recesses of my subconscious, forbidding it to rear its head any time soon. Or at least not until I'm alone.

Michael takes us to a fast-food joint and gets us both an ice cream cone. We don't speak on the way back to the house.

Finally, we pull into the driveway, and Michael puts the truck in park.

"Well, here we are again," he says with a smile.

"Here we are again," I repeat.

"You gonna be okay?" he asks.

"I'll be fine," I tell him. "I'm about to text Jackie and tell her to bring Olivia back. Maybe she'll stay a little while," I suggest, more for his sake than mine. I don't want him to think I'm going to spend the afternoon being sad. Even if Jackie doesn't stay, I definitely won't be upset about it. I can handle it.

"You're always such a tough cookie," Michael says with a sad chuckle. "You know it's okay to be vulnerable with people?"

This makes me bristle, a memory coming to me—many memories—of times that Michael said this to me when we were married. It was something we fought about constantly. He wanted more than I could give him emotionally. And I just couldn't let that wall come all the way down.

"We're not married anymore, Michael," I remind him.

My words are icy, venomous. When I look at Michael

and see his expression, I know they landed just as I intended. I hurt his feelings.

I climb out of the truck and slam the door, heading for the house.

AFTER ABOUT TEN MINUTES, Jackie pulls into the drive with her topless Mustang, Olivia in the passenger seat, a huge smile on her face. I mirror the expression as I watch them through the dining-room window. Olivia deserves a moment of freedom. The kind you can only get driving across town, mid-summer, in a convertible with the top down.

Because I don't imagine that her life is going to have much more of that for a while.

The thought comes back to me that this may already be spreading as a rumor. There may already be parents talking about it, their kids listening. All of it getting back to Olivia in ugly ways. The thought turns my stomach. I'll hate myself forever.

I swing the door open as the two of them are coming up the sidewalk.

"There she is," I say to Olivia.

Her smile almost instantly fades, but a hint of it remains, and she offers that to me.

I pat her shoulder, and she walks past me, already heading for her bedroom.

"There she is," Jackie echoes my words, saying them softly but looking at me.

She wraps me in a hug. Her body is soft, comforting.

I could stay in her embrace forever. The thought is dangerous; I know.

"Come in," I whisper.

Jackie lets go of me and heads into the house, and a sweet smell trails after her. I inhale it, trying to brand the scent into my brain.

I shut the door, and Jackie takes a seat at the bar.

"White wine, please," she says. "Oh, what am I saying?" She gets up and goes to the fridge. "I should be serving you."

She winks at me, and it sends butterflies swirling around my stomach.

She goes to the fridge and gets two wine glasses. She pours us both some and hands me mine. This time I go around to sit at the bar. Jackie leans against it at the end, only about a foot from me.

"How are you holding up?" she asks.

"I'm fine," I tell her. It's not a total lie.

In some ways.

I sigh.

"Underwood is kind of breathing down my neck," I say.

"Have you not told him about the stuff I gave you?" Jackie asks. "If you won't, I will, Kim."

"I haven't. But I'm going to. Things have been pretty hostile between the two of us. I think he's convinced I did it. I'm not sure he'll even listen if I tell him what you found. Maybe it would be better coming from you," I suggest.

The idea makes sense, giving me some bit of comfort.

Maybe he would listen to Jackie.

I can see him blowing past it, thinking that I'm trying to send him out chasing a red herring.

Underwood seems like the kind of detective that decides about how a crime played out and no amount of evidence can change his mind. You read about that stuff all the time. Crimes where the police were so convinced that it went one way, only for the public to find out decades later that the wrong person has been in prison the whole time.

That wrong person might be me in this case.

The thought replaces the butterflies in my stomach with serpents, rearing their heads and snapping up any of the remaining benevolent bugs.

"I can do that," Jackie says. "You got it, sweetie."

She places a hand on my leg and it lingers there for a moment. I feel my cheeks heat up.

I look over at her.

She's so beautiful.

She downs the rest of her glass of wine.

"Want more?" She removes her hand from my thigh and points at her glass.

"I'm good," I say. I've still got a lot left. Alcohol just doesn't seem like the best thing for my stomach right now. I need something more like chicken broth. Something that would settle it.

"So, how was it today?" Jackie asks, referring to the funeral arrangements.

"Not bad," I say. "Michael went with me. We got into a...little disagreement when he dropped me off, though." I take a sip of wine, trying to force myself to relax.

"What was it about?" Jackie probes, coming back with her full glass.

"Nothing important," I say. I don't want to get into it with Jackie. Not right now. Right now, I just want her to stay here as long as possible.

"Oh, I see," she teases. "You think he's still in love with you?" she asks.

I look at her, taken aback by the question. I've never mentioned it to Jackie, but she has a way of seeing through people. And she's been around Michael a few times. I've never thought he was that transparent, but maybe he is.

"I don't know," I say. "Maybe."

"Are you still in love with him?" she asks, arching an eyebrow. She takes a sip of her wine and maintains eye contact with me. The butterflies are back.

"No," I mumble.

"That would be a shame if you were," Jackie returns.

Her eyes are half-lidded, sultry. She's enjoying this. That I'm shifting in my seat, unable to keep looking her in the eye. I wonder if it's just a game for her. I clear my throat, not wanting to go any further down that path.

"Jackie," I say. "Is there anything else you know?"

Now it's Jackie's turn to shift uncomfortably. Which I wasn't expecting.

"No," she says simply, but the word is a little too short. Like she doesn't trust herself to say more.

"If you know anything, I need to know," I say.

I watch as she swallows. I wonder if her mouth has gone dry. She takes a sip of wine, probably to avoid having to speak.

"I know nothing but what I told you," she says, looking me in the eye. But it's like she had a take a moment to screw up the courage to do that. Like she couldn't have done it right after I asked the question.

I look at her. Jackie's gorgeous. And there's no denying that I find her attractive. But I don't think she's being entirely honest with me.

I struggle for words, unsure of what to say next. I let it die, leaving the conversation to her.

"I'm glad you're okay," she finally says.

I nod halfheartedly. *Am I okay?*

"It's such a crazy situation," Jackie goes on. "I promise I'll call Detective Underwood and tell him about the note and that you told me you saw them buying burner phones," she says.

"Maybe you should say that you saw Amanda doing that," I suggest.

"Probably a good idea," she says. "I don't know how well it would work in your favor if Underwood just thinks we're playing telephone and manipulating him.

"Me, either."

"I can get out of your hair," Jackie says.

"You're not in my hair," I say with a chuckle.

I don't want her to leave. I stand, though, and walk to the door with her after she downs the rest of her wine.

"You okay to drive?" I ask.

"Fine," she assures me.

She wraps me in another hug and then pulls away slightly where we're facing each other, her nose only a few inches from mine. I smell the sweet mint on her breath again. My heart stops. The moment stretches on endlessly. And then Jackie pulls all the way away and slips out the front door.

I say nothing, but I know two things.
I would have kissed her.
And she knows *something*.

FIFTEEN

BILLY'S BODY is ready for the visitation that night.

It's so strange to think about it that way. His body.

Not him.

Not anymore.

I dress in slacks and a blouse. I look the part of the grieving widow. Everything's black, including my shoes. I emerge from the bedroom and head down the hall in my monochromatic ensemble, and I find Olivia perched on a barstool playing on her phone.

"You ready?" I ask.

"Yeah," she says without looking up from the app that's got her attention.

"What are you looking at?" I ask her.

She locks her phone instantly and shoots me a glare. Her eyes are bloodshot, red around the rim. She's been crying.

"Olivia, what's wrong?" I ask.

"Nothing, I'm fine, Mom," she says.

She stands up and heads for her bedroom.

"We need to leave here in, like, two minutes," I holler after her.

She raises a hand and waves it back at me, acknowledging the request, though I'm not sure if she'll honor it.

I give her more like ten minutes and finally, she comes down the hallway looking less like the girl that had been crying only a little while ago. I want to ask her again what's wrong. To probe further.

"Olivia," I say as we get into the SUV.

"I'm fine, Mom, really," she says preemptively.

"You can talk to me, Liv," I tell her, backing the car out onto the street. I head for the main road that leads into town.

"I know," she says.

But it's curt. There's something about it that lets me know she most definitely does not think she can talk to me. Not about this and not about anything.

"Olivia," I say more sternly, trying my best. "Please, talk to me."

"I don't fucking want to, Mom!" She shouts it at me.

I'm startled into silence. I don't tell her not to cuss at me. Now's not the time to tell her that her anger is misplaced. I'm too stunned.

Olivia has always been a good kid. She's never gotten into trouble at school.

"I know you loved your step-dad," I say. "And it's okay for you to be mad that he died."

Olivia sniffles in the passenger seat, her face turned away from me as she leans her forehead against the window. I feel the weight of her crying in the silence between us.

I speak again.

"I loved him, too," I say.

"No, you didn't," she spins quickly and bites the words off.

Once again, I'm shocked.

I look at her, staring a little too long as we go down the road.

"Mom!" Olivia points to the road ahead and I whip my head around right before I'm about to plow us into the back of a semi-truck. I slam on the brakes and we jolt forward. Both of us are silent. The reality of what almost happened seems to wash over us in that moment.

We drive to the funeral home without a word after that.

I think about Olivia's words as we get out of the SUV. The sun sets across the cemetery and I look at it. I want to think I'm looking at the sunset because it's beautiful, and it's nice to focus on a beautiful thing before you have to see something ugly. But that's not it at all. I'm looking out across the cemetery to see if the black sedan is here.

And there it is. I see it sitting across the cemetery, reminding me of a lion on the savannah waiting for a weak gazelle to stray from the herd.

When I look back at the building, there are no cars that I recognize. We're here early enough that we'll have some time to ourselves in the stateroom. The sedan leaves me with an uneasy feeling, though.

I'm not looking forward to the time alone with Olivia. Not after the drive.

We walk in and Amy, the girl from earlier, leads us to the stateroom.

As she's about to leave us alone, she says something to me.

"Is your—" she cuts off immediately.

"My ex-husband," I say for her. "Yeah, he'll be here."

I give her a sharp-edged smile, inviting no further small talk.

"I'll be out at the front if you need me," she says, then turns, giving the impression of an animal scurrying away with its tail tucked.

I turn back around, and there's Billy's casket. I can see his face just poking out of it against the white linen backdrop that has a white cross embroidered on it. The image is almost laughable, I think. Billy might have been conservative, but he wasn't religious. Well, he was sometimes. When it suited him.

It was all about appearances. Which, I suppose, makes the cross rather fitting. The last visual he'll put out on earth before he's buried six feet under it.

The thought is bitter. I'm bitter.

I walk closer to the casket, forgetting Olivia for a moment. I approach it, place my hand on the cool steel of the bottom portion that's closed across his legs. I wonder if he's really wearing the shoes I gave them. Maybe some intern made off with them. I've heard horror stories of such things. But if anyone deserves their shoes stolen before they make their journey into the afterlife, it's Billy.

I imagine him walking in sock feet over the fiery coals of hell.

His face is made up, caked so that you can't see the bruising that was there. But if you'd seen it the other night, you can still see it now. He looks unnatural, that side of his face a little puffy. I reach out to touch it and his flesh is cold and doughy like a sculptor's clay.

I feel nothing but resentment.

Resentment because he didn't live long enough for me to have been the one that left. I wanted to know that I could walk away from my marriage with him. That I wasn't just another woman stuck. I'd never thought of myself that way, but now, looking at him lying dead in a casket, I'm not sure I was ever anything else.

I turn back.

"Oliv—" I stop short. She's gone from the room.

I drop my hand from Billy's casket, and I walk to the door. I peer out into the hallway, but I don't see her in either direction. I step outside of the room and listen, straining my ears to hear where she might be. It reminds me for a moment of when she was a toddler. How no noise meant she was up to something. I'm not sure much has changed.

I head down the hallway toward the lobby of the funeral home. I spot Amy sitting at her computer, working away, and I walk up.

"Excuse me, Amy," I say. "Have you seen my daughter?" I ask.

Amy looks up at me, still wary of me after our encounter a few moments earlier.

"I haven't," she says with doe-eyed innocence.

I nod and thank her. I walk around to the other side where the chapel is. Glancing in, I don't see Olivia's ponytail sticking up anywhere in the pews. I sigh, exasperated, and head out the opposite end of the sanctuary, out a door and into a hallway.

It's quickly clear that this is a staff only portion of the building. I slow my steps and still my breath, feeling like I'm trespassing. It would be highly unlikely that Olivia would be anywhere that would require breaking the rules.

But even as the thought crosses my mind, I hear something around the corner again. The opening and closing of a door. My gut tells me it's Olivia, but my intellect tells me I'm going to get in trouble for being back here and it's most likely a funeral director.

Oh, well. I'll tell them I can't find my daughter.

I march to the end of the hallway and turn into the next corridor. And there I see a door that says PREPARATION ROOM.

I press my ear to the door, hesitant to open it. Not because I'm afraid of getting in trouble for wandering where I'm not supposed to, but afraid of what I might see when I open it.

I hear a sniffle, then a soft cry that I recognize instantly.

I throw the door open.

"Olivia!" I say with a gasp when I take it what's on the other side of that door.

I see my daughter standing over a body not a year older than her own. A little girl, dead and cold on a table. On the side of her temple is a very clean hole that I can only imagine marks the entrance to the pathway that a bullet took through her brain.

Olivia chokes back a sob.

"I didn't mean to come in here!" Olivia cries to me.

She runs and wraps her arms around me.

"Olivia, it's okay," I tell her, not mad. Only horrified that my daughter saw such a thing.

I stroke her hair and gently walk her out of the room, closing the door behind us.

"She even looked like me," she sobs.

"Baby, it's okay," I tell her. "It's horribly, horribly sad. And it's okay to feel sad about it. But it's not you," I tell her, promise in my voice.

"It could be." Olivia looks up at me with tears streaming down her face and a little snot dripping from her nose. I'm instantly transported back to the time that she popped a wheelie and fell off her bike, breaking her wrist.

The way she had sobbed. It was like the keening cry of a wounded animal. A sound that a mother could never forget. She seems on the verge of that now.

"Baby, it's okay," I tell her, wrapping her tightly in my arms. She allows this. A sure sign that Olivia isn't in a good place. I guess in my emotional distance from Billy, I didn't realize how much it could hurt the daughter that loved him.

If he could only be good to one of us, at least it was her.

The thought dances through my mind. It's the truth. I wouldn't want it any other way. But suddenly, I'm wishing I'd never met the man. That this had all never come to pass. That Olivia wasn't hurting like this.

"It's okay," I repeat to her in the hallway.

After she calms down, I lead her back out to the chapel and to the lobby of the funeral home.

We reach the state-room door.

"I don't want to go in there," Olivia says. "I don't want to see him like that."

Tears threaten to spill out of her eyes once more.

I nod and step inside for a moment to grab my keys.

"You can sit in the car if you'd like, honey. I'll have your daddy come pick you up."

She nods and heads for the car while I make a call to Michael.

SIXTEEN

MICHAEL SHOWS up about fifteen minutes later, and it's about ten minutes before everyone else is set to come down to the funeral home. He calls me when he gets to the parking lot. I walk outside to meet him as he gets out of his truck.

"Where is she?" he asks.

"In the SUV," I tell him, arms crossed over my chest.

"Is she okay?" he asks.

"I think this is hitting her harder than I thought it would," I tell him. "They were really close, you know? She's pretty upset."

"And you say she saw a dead body?" Michael asks. "Like, other than Billy's?"

"A teenage girl. She snuck into the preparation area in the back. I found her. She was sobbing. This girl had shot herself in the head, apparently. I think Olivia is dealing with a lot of emotions right now. Plus, she's a teenager," I say.

"Jesus Christ. That's an image she won't forget any time soon," Michael says.

Then his gaze lingers on me.

"What about you?" he asks. "How're you holding up, honey?"

The pet name is one he rarely uses. Maybe twice since our divorce. I would correct him, but tonight I let it slide. It feels nice to know he cares.

"I'm okay," I tell him, too tired to be on the defensive. Too tired to make sure he stays outside the walls I've so expertly built. Part of me wants someone inside of them right now. Someone that can tell me everything's going to be alright. And Michael's familiar, and all too willing to be that person for me.

I would never take advantage of him that way, though.

I couldn't.

He steps forward and brushes a lock of hair out of my face that I didn't realize had fallen.

"You look tired," he says.

"I am tired," I tell him with a laugh, but it doesn't reach my eyes. It stops short, halfhearted, and overshadowed because Detective Underwood thinks I'm the one who set this all into motion.

"You ever call that cop about the stuff you found out?" Michael asks.

"No. But Jackie's going to," I tell him.

"Probably better that way," Michael says. "If he suspects you and all."

"That he does," I tell him.

"Kim," he says. "If there's anything at all that I can

do, please call me. I don't care what time it is." There's a pleading in his eyes. A willingness and a desire to help me however he can. I want to let him. I need to let him.

But there's a part of me that just can't.

I can handle this on my own.

"I'm okay, Michael," I say. I smile up at him, somewhat sadly.

It's a shame things went the way they went. Michael didn't want a divorce, but I couldn't stand to let him be devoted to me when I didn't want to be monogamous with him. He didn't care, he'd said. He would have burnt and salted the earth for me.

I try to remember what it felt to be loved like that.

Because I hadn't known it in a long time.

I'M in the state room alone for almost exactly one minute when someone comes to the door with a gentle knock. I expect Amy or Derek. Maybe someone to see if I want a glass of water. But instead, it's Jackie and I beam at her.

I get up and we hug. She wraps me up tightly and I inhale the scent of her.

She smells the way I thought heaven would when I was a teenager.

Now I'm not so sure that there is a heaven.

Or a hell.

Or any kind of real justice in this world.

She smiles back at me.

"Hey, gorgeous," she says, placing a kiss on my cheek. "You doing okay?"

"I'm fine," I tell her. It's pretty much true. Other than being worried about Olivia, I am fine. Oh, and worrying about going to jail. "Did you—"

"I called and left an anonymous tip today," Jackie says in a whisper.

I nod my head, hoping that it already made its way to Underwood.

"Do you think they'll come?" Jackie asks, meaning Dan and Amanda.

"I don't know," I say.

Just then, Nathan steps into the room and offers me a pressed smile, a nod, and a wave. I wave back, but turn my focus on Jackie.

"If I was guilty of murder, I would show up tonight," Jackie says. "I wouldn't want anyone to be suspicious."

My gaze lingers on her, studying her for a moment.

"Do you think so?" I ask. "I would probably make an excuse and not come," I say.

"And that's why I would be a better criminal than you, Thelma," she says with a wink.

I laugh despite being in a room with my husband's cold, dead body.

Maybe she's right. Maybe they will show up tonight.

Maybe they won't, though.

Which would be smarter? Which would be worse?

I don't know.

The only thing I know for sure is that someone there that night had something to do with this. Someone I know pretty well, at that. Or at least that I thought knew pretty well.

Anger swells in my chest, thinking about Olivia

today. Whoever killed Billy set that in motion. They'd created the atmosphere in which Olivia was falling apart.

And I find myself furious about it.

"Well," I say. "I guess we'll find out."

Jackie nods.

"We will," she says.

Everyone else gets there a little later. Nicole offers me a weak hug. Amanda does the same. I can tell there's an awkwardness to everything now. Fixing it is going to be impossible, I know that. For now, I'm just grateful they're all here.

WE ARE ALONE for about five minutes. And then people pour in.

I shake hands with at least ten people that Billy managed money for. All of them have nothing but glowing things to say about my late husband. How good he was with money. How funny and charming he was. What a delight he was to work with.

Billy doesn't have much family. There was a rift long ago that never healed. So it doesn't surprise me when none of them show up.

Friends of Billy's through work show up as well.

Again, nothing but wonderful things to say about him.

I think that there must be something wrong with me since, apparently, I feel like it's okay to speak ill of the dead.

What does it matter? It's the truth.

People speak in soft conversations, smiles and laughs are exchanged even in the presence of a dead body. It's so strange, I think. Anglo-Saxon-Protestants are the most clinical about grief. Like it's this thing that needs to be compartmentalized and kept from bleeding into the other aspects of life. If there are any tears, they are muted, sobbed into tissues and covered up by an embrace so no one else will see or hear.

I seethe, thinking about Olivia earlier.

The image of that stark, clean entry wound will stay with me forever, I imagine.

And I imagine it will also stay with Olivia forever.

I hope that she and her dad got pizza and are knee deep in video games right now. I hope that he's making her laugh, making her forget for a little while. Maybe things seem normal to her. She deserves normal.

I dread taking her back to school.

I want to keep her safe. And once she's at school, I can't protect her.

The thought is sickening.

I wish I was with her right now, somewhere far away from this. In some other universe where we're able to really talk to each other. When this is all over, I'm going to therapy. And it might not hurt for Olivia to go, too.

For now, it's too much to think about.

For now, all we need to do is survive. And I'm good at surviving.

I clear my throat, sitting alone for a moment on the couch across the room from Billy's open casket.

"Excuse me," a woman says.

I spin to face her.

"Are you Kim?" the woman asks.

She's about my age and has lanky features, far too thin and tall. And she looks pained to be here.

"Yes," I say, almost hesitantly.

"I'm Lindsay," she says, sticking out her hand. "Lindsay Karlsen. Billy's sister."

You could knock me over where I stand with just the push of a finger.

Billy's sister.

I wasn't even aware that such a relative existed. Billy had never mentioned her.

"I know this is strange," she says. "But I just had to see him."

"Of course," I say, almost breathless. I have so many things I want to ask her, but I refrain.

"I'm sorry to just show up here without calling you, but I thought it might be better that way. I didn't want you to stress about it. I really just want to see him and see how you're doing," she says.

"Of course," I echo myself, unable to come up with another similar sentence.

She gives me a sad smile and is about to excuse herself, but then I find my tongue.

"You two were estranged," I say, more a statement than a question as I put the pieces together in my head.

"We were," Lindsay says. "It just sort of...happened," she explains. "I'm sure he told you all about that before you got married, though. I don't need to dredge it up now on an already unpleasant night," she says with a dark chuckle.

"Right," I say, though I'm totally unsure of what she's

referring to. The most that Billy ever told me was that he wasn't close with his family and that he didn't want to talk about it more than that.

I have no idea of anything else.

Lindsay steps away and heads to the casket. I fight with the urge to follow her. I want to ask her what she meant, but I don't want to seem like an idiot.

She obviously thinks I already know about whatever it is.

My mind whirls, speculating wildly about what it could be. What happened between them?

Why would Billy not tell me?

I realize my heart is beating faster when Jackie comes over and taps me on the shoulder. I startle, turning to face her as quickly as I might an attacker in a dark alleyway.

"Whoa, you alright?" Jackie asks, taken a little aback by my reaction.

"I'm fine," I say, then take a deep breath.

"Who was that?" Jackie asks.

"Billy's sister, of all people," I tell Jackie.

Jackie looks over at her, standing next to Billy's casket, having her own private moment with her deceased brother.

"I thought he didn't have any family," Jackie says.

"I thought he didn't, either," I say.

"Weird," Jackie says. "Grief makes people do strange things."

"That's for sure," I say.

Before the night is over, Lindsay comes to see me again when I'm not talking to anyone else. I'm emotionally exhausted, ready to go home.

"Kim," she says, fishing out a notebook and a pen. "I want you to have this if you ever want to call me about anything."

She scribbles something on the paper and then hands it to me.

It's her phone number.

"Thank you," I say, energy flickering through me.

"Of course," she says, sounding like me when I first met her, though I can tell she means it. Then she disappears out into the hallway.

I rub my thumb over the drying ink and smear it slightly when I do.

I do have questions for her.

SEVENTEEN

OLIVIA SEEMS to make it a point to be as polite as she can to me the morning of the funeral. She makes me breakfast and pours me a glass of orange juice when I first emerge from my bedroom. I smile at her effort.

"Olivia, you don't need to do all this," I say.

"I just wanted to do something nice for you today," she whispers, looking down.

I let her have the moment, not dissuading her from her intent.

"Thank you," I say softly and then sip my orange juice.

With the funeral over today, it'll be time to talk to Olivia about going back to school. The thought still fills me with dread. I don't even want to consider it. I want to protect her. Like I could when she was growing inside me.

I know that's not the real world, though.

I feel powerless over what will happen once she goes

back to school. This town talks, and gossip travels. I wonder if one cop told his wife, who told her friend, who told her nanny, who told her grandmother, who spread it at church, and so on and so forth.

I saw the way they looked at us that night. Like they knew what kind of people we were when they knew nothing about any of us.

I get ready with all of this in mind, putting me in a gray mood before I even step foot into the chapel. Michael shows up around 9:15 to pick us up. The service starts at 10:00 at the funeral home. Billy never went to church and only cited the Bible when judging others, and I'm not religious. It didn't feel right to have it anywhere but on neutral ground. Besides, I might burst into flames if I set foot in a church.

We pull up outside of Pickard and Sons. They pulled the hearse under the awning that leads into the atrium of the sanctuary. Large doors are ready to open up and let a casket roll through, right into the back of the waiting transport.

The three of us get out of the truck and on the sidewalk, I straighten the jacket of my suit. Once again, all black. The picture of the grieving widow. Right down to the giant shades on my face that people will think are meant to hide my tears, when actually, they're to hide the fact that I'm not crying at all.

I pat Olivia on the back as she steps up onto the sidewalk.

"You okay, kiddo?" I ask.

"I'm fine," she says.

Her voice is hollowed out. Like she's tucked her emotions deep down beneath the marrow and muscles in her body, back into some mystical, ancient place that no surgeon would ever find.

That her mother would never find, either.

"Come on," I say with a smile, pushing her gently to walk in front of me.

When we arrive, no one's here. Derek, the funeral director, ushers us into the family room.

It's a giant space, empty as a drum. Or at least it feels giant when you have no family in it with you. Just me, my kid, and my ex-husband on the day of my current husband's funeral. It almost seems like a joke.

For a second, I wonder if Lindsay will come in here with us. And I'm filled with a desire to tell her she should. I step out into the hall and see Derek waiting at the door to greet people. I walk over to him.

"Excuse me," I say.

"Yes, ma'am," Derek says, turning his full attention to me.

"There's a woman. Tall and thin with brown hair about down to here," I point at my shoulder. "Her name is Lindsay, and she's my sister-in-law." The phrase feels awkward on my tongue, but I go with it. "Please tell her she should come in and wait with us."

"Of course, ma'am. I'll find her," he says with a solemn nod.

I turn to head back to the family room, satisfied that Derek takes his job seriously, even if he seemed like he might have been judging us the other day.

Who could blame him? I would do the same thing if I were in his position.

Michael and Olivia get started playing a game on Michael's phone, taking turns. They're lost in their own little world. I keep pacing to the door, watching through the tiny window next to it as people pour into the chapel, all of them filing into the pews in the sanctuary.

I smile back at Olivia and Michael each time that I turn back. I walk over and then pace again, like a bear in a too-small enclosure at a zoo.

I head for the door again and just before I reach it, the handle turns and it opens.

Lindsay peers around it.

"Am I in the right place?" she asks, somewhat meekly.

"You are," I tell her with a smile. "Come in."

I hesitate, but after she closes the door behind herself, I offer her a hug. She accepts gladly and the two of us stand there in an embrace for several seconds. She rubs her hand against my upper back in comforting circles.

"Come, sit," I say, breaking away from her.

I indicate two chairs at the opposite end from where Michael and Olivia are engrossed in their game. Michael looks over, curious about the strange woman in the room with us. She glances at him too and offers him an awkward, pressed smile.

I want a moment to talk to Lindsay, my curiosity getting the best of me. I need to know more about what she said before. About why Billy stopped talking to his family.

I wonder if they shared a domineering father. If Billy

never followed in footsteps he was expected to. If he wasn't the golden child. Maybe it was the mother. A series of scenarios race through my head.

"How are you?" Lindsay asks, catching me off guard. Left to my own devices, I might have just dived into the questions about Billy's past.

"I'm alright," I tell her, honestly. "To be perfectly honest with you, things weren't great at the end."

Lindsay nods.

"Billy could be a difficult man to live with," she says. "I remember."

"How so?" I try to press gently, but it comes off too inquisitive even to my ears.

"Billy could be difficult," Lindsay says. I can tell she's treading carefully, probably so she won't inadvertently upset me. I want to tell her we're beyond that point. I say nothing instead. "Or at least he was when I was still in his life," she adds.

I glance over my shoulder at Olivia and Michael, making sure they're buried in computer-generated images and renderings of their favorite heroes and villains. They seem happy doing their thing. In other words, they aren't bothering to listen to this conversation.

Good.

"What happened with Billy and the family?" I ask.

Lindsay's expression changes.

"He never told you?" she asks, her words tentative, like she's creeping through a jungle avoiding landmines.

"No," I say.

Lindsay swallows, clears her throat and stands.

"It's not right to speak ill of the dead," she says. "I should go."

And then she heads for the door and lets herself out.

I watch as it closes behind her, and I wonder what the hell happened inside that family.

THE SERVICE GOES off without a hitch. I spot our friends in the crowd. I don't have a lot of time to look at them, though. Nicole catches my eye right before we sit down and offers me a comforting smile. We haven't spoken since it happened. It's like no one really knows what to say.

I think about every true crime documentary I've watched where the killer returns to the scene of the crime or shows up at a funeral or vigil for the victim.

Isn't that common?

Could they be here?

After the funeral, we head to the graveside. Michael, Olivia, and I emerge from the family car. There's a great, green awning over the grave, blocking out the noon-day July sun in Texas. Underneath, astroturf has been draped everywhere, disguising the ugly, torn earth that Billy's casket is going to be lowered into. The whole thing is as antiseptic as possible. So far from reality, all the way from the makeup to the Superbowl-worthy fake grass.

Green velvet lines two rows of folding chairs. The two rows only make it clear that neither my family nor Billy's are attending. When I look out into the crowd to invite Lindsay to sit next to us, I don't find her.

I wonder if she left after the service, not wanting to see me again.

I wouldn't blame her. I made her uncomfortable.

I sigh to myself and settle into my seat. I catch sight, out of the corner of my eye, of a car that just pulled up. And I recognize the suited man that emerges immediately.

Detective Underwood.

I bristle at the sight of him.

I want to tell him he's not welcome here. Not so much for the sanctity of Billy's service, but because looking at him makes anger boil over inside of me. He believes I did this. I doubt he's even bothered with the tip that Jackie called in.

I glance around behind us and see Dan and Amanda.

Jason and Nicole are next to them.

I seethe, thinking about Underwood, turning back to face the casket with a straight back. I hold my head high. I had nothing to do with this and I'll be damned if he cows me into acting like I did. He can cuff me and take me downtown all he wants, but it doesn't change the fact that I'm innocent.

Bastard.

Out of the corner of my eye, I see him sidle up to the tent, barely out of my line of vision.

He's fucking with me.

Just then, the chaplain comes up to the graveside, holding a book in his hands that I'm sure is the Bible. Probably the King James Version, if I know anything about where I'm living. He doesn't open it when he speaks, though. Just as I requested.

"Good afternoon, folks," he says. "As we lay William Karlsen to rest today, let's take a moment of silence and think about all the memories we have of him. Send out healing and hope to his family and friends, and reflect on what a life well-lived really is."

He bows his head as if in prayer and the crowd, chittering moments before, goes deadly silent.

Michael reaches across Olivia's lap and grabs my hand, squeezing it.

I look up and notice Underwood watching us. I make eye contact with him and squeeze Michael's hand. I don't look away until the chaplain speaks again.

"We are gathered to honor a husband, father, and friend today," he says.

I tune him out as he goes on briefly. He doesn't take long. All I can think about is Underwood standing off to the side, here to irritate me rather than do his job. My vision blurs at the edges as the anger bubbles up harder and harder, reaching a boiling point soon.

The chaplain concludes the service and people start talking again. Olivia asks if she can have one of the flowers from the spray on his casket.

"Of course," Michael says. "We can press it and you can keep it."

Olivia smiles at her dad, and his genuine compassion for her brings me back down to earth.

Michael never felt threatened by Billy, even if he teased me about him. He never tried to make Olivia feel like she needed to choose. He knew he was her father and no one could ever compete with that position. Michael is a wonderful dad. And he wasn't a bad husband. Not at all. It was me that wasn't a suitable partner. And God bless him, he would have stayed if I'd have let him.

Olivia picks her flower and I see Underwood watching her from the side of the tent. I stand up, straighten my suit, and head over to him.

"Hello, Mrs. Karlsen," he says, his southern accent mellifluous and full of venom at the same time.

"Detective Underwood," I say. "I'm going to assume this isn't a visit for your health. What brings you to my husband's funeral?"

Underwood hesitates at first. I grind my teeth.

"You seem stressed, Kimberly," he says, using my first name. It irritates me.

"I'm fine," I assure him, though my words come out too sharply for that to be the case.

"Good, good," Underwood says. "I would assume on a day like this that you'd be too distraught to hold it together."

"What are you saying? Are you upset? Because I'm not crying and doing what you think a widow should do?" I snap back at him. "You didn't know the inside of my marriage, Detective."

"Indeed," he says. "But I intend to."

His words are cool, collected. It inflames me more.

"Listen," I say, turning to face him. "I don't know why you've got this burr under your saddle about me and think that I did this. Because I didn't. And even if you put me on trial for it, I still didn't do it and the person who did is out there. Or maybe even here," I say, raising my voice and throwing my arms in the air. "Did you think of that? Or did you entirely ignore what my friend Jackie called to tell you?" I regret my words instantly, but they're already out of my mouth.

"So, that was Jackie that called in the tip?" Underwood asks, entirely ignoring everything else I've said.

"That's not the point! Have you even looked into it?!"

"I find it interesting that your friend would call in a tip about what she saw at the super center when you're the one who was there that day. We have you on video at the checkout," he says.

"Oh, fuck you," I spit.

"You need to calm down," Underwood says seriously.

"No. Fuck. You. Troy," I say. "You're not doing your goddamned job." My voice raises. I'm yelling now. People stop talking. "You need to fucking investigate Daniel and Amanda Blankenship and find out why the fuck they bought burner phones right after my husband died."

Underwood is silent.

My friends are silent, watching me turn on them right here in broad daylight. I glance over at them, Dan and Amanda, Jason and Nicole. Everyone is taken aback. I've become a pestilence. None of them will touch me again. Not with their hands, not with their hearts.

"Come with me," he says. He spins me roughly and cuffs me immediately.

"You can't arrest me!" I shout.

Underwood marches me to his car and throws me in the backseat, slamming the door.

I scream and kick the seat in front of me. I throw my head back against the headrest, writhing and yelling, appalled at this. It's outrageous.

"Michael!" I yell.

Michael and Olivia come over to talk to Underwood but Underwood seems to dismiss them. Finally, another familiar face comes over. And to my surprise, it's the man I just pointed at.

Dan.

He talks to Underwood, pointing at me in the car. I watch as the two of them go back and forth. Underwood doesn't look upset. In fact, I think Dan is calming him down. Amanda watches from the edge of the crowd, her face unreadable.

Dan shakes hands with Underwood and Underwood turns, opens the door to the back of the car.

"Come on," he says, reaching in for me. He grabs my arm roughly and pulls me out, pinching my skin.

I shake him off as I stand on the grass. Dan looks at me, his gaze steely.

Underwood uncuffs me and I get away from him as fast as I can. I straighten my clothes and look at him.

"You don't know what you're doing," I tell Underwood.

He just stares at me, a smirk on his face.

"You need to thank your friend here," he says, gesturing at Dan.

I look between the both of them. Ungrateful for either.

Underwood walks around his car and gets in without another word. He starts it up and pulls away from the funeral procession. I watch him go. Then Dan speaks.

"Stay the fuck away from us," he says, a razor's edge to his voice.

I stare at him, wondering if this is the same man I knew just a few days ago.

He spins and heads back to Amanda.

I look over at her, looking for the people I thought were my friends.

She sneers, and the two of them disappear into the crowd.

EIGHTEEN

IF I WERE A CARTOON, steam would shoot out of my ears as I walk up to Michael.

"Are you okay?" he asks, suddenly going into protector mode.

"I'm fine," I say. "I think he just wanted to scare me." I calm down slightly.

Even if I don't want to admit it, Michael has a calming effect on me. I look up at him. His eyes are kind, worried. I glance at Olivia. She's shocked silent, unsure of how to process what her mom just did. A terrible thought occurs to me. That I might have frightened her.

I turn my focus to my daughter.

"Honey," I say. "Everything's okay. That detective is looking in all the wrong places to find out what happened to Billy."

Olivia looks at me, concern on her face.

"I promise I won't lose my temper like that again," I tell her.

She nods her head absently. I want to drown myself in a bottle of whiskey.

I can't believe I did that in front of my daughter. I probably just made everything about all of this a hundred times worse for her. Now, not only will the gossip mill be talking about the possibility that Kim Karlsen was the one who killed her husband, they might also talk about what kind of parties Kim Karlsen throws at her house.

And that's the last kind of rumor that Olivia needs to be dealing with at school.

A scream begs to rip from my lungs. I need it to tear through the air like the sound of a keening animal. I feel lost. A feeling that I've only had in life a few times and one that I don't care to have again.

I take a moment to look around at the dwindling crowd. People have scattered, heading to their cars. None of them wanting to be present for another meltdown. All of them probably thinking I had something to do with Billy's death now.

"Shit," I say under my breath. "Shit! Shit! SHIT!"

"Hey," Michael says, placing a hand on the side of my face. I look up at him. It's like he can read my mind. "Since when have you cared what anyone thinks?"

I never have, but this is different. This time, it's about our daughter.

I don't tell him that, though. Even if I did, there's nothing he can do to stop the rumor mill or shield Olivia or me from any of it.

I sigh and smile at Michael. He means well. Michael's like a golden retriever. I think that's what Olivia's generation says. He has that wholesome energy even if he was married to me at one point. My mind drifts, thinking about how things might be now if I'd let him convince me not to file for divorce.

The thought brings with it a warm, comforting feeling that covers me like a blanket. Welcome even in this heat.

"Why don't we get out of here?" Michael says.

"I think that's a good idea," I say. "You ready, kiddo?"

Olivia nods her head, but it's her expression that worries me. It's one that she shouldn't have to wear. One that should belong to someone far older, my mother or my sister, not my daughter.

She's concerned about me.

I want to tell her I'm okay. She's okay. Everything's going to be okay.

But I don't know that for sure.

The thought makes the warmth I previously felt disappear, like the first gust of an icy front rolling into town on a late spring day, heralding the possibility of a bad storm.

We all walk over to the family car, ready to go back to the funeral home. And we pile in.

Most of the people have left the cemetery. The ones still here are clustered in little groups of three or four looking like the little groups of ducks that inhabit the graveyard. I wonder for a moment if they're all talking about what just happened.

I sigh and sit back in my seat.

Maybe I shouldn't care what they think. I know the truth. I did nothing wrong.

I start thinking about Billy's sister. That he even had

a sister, and I never knew anything about her bothers me a lot. Like an awful lot. I can't imagine why he'd want to keep something like that from me.

Then again, I'm not close with my family. And Billy always said things were strained with he and his.

I can wrap my mind around that.

Still. I think about calling his sister.

The driver from the funeral home gets into the front seat of the car and we take off. I glance out the window at the remaining people in the cemetery one last time. I wonder what all of them make of the situation. If they blame me. If they could think I had anything to do with this.

Underwood certainly does.

My mind drifts to other things, exhaustion taking over. But it's short-lived when I catch something out of the corner of my eye.

A black sedan, pulling even with us at a stoplight, the windows tinted so dark that I'd never be able to make out who was inside even if I wanted to. A chill runs through me and I sit up straighter.

I peer out the window, stare, really. My eyes probe the darkness. Even in the mid-day summer sun, I can't tell if it's a man or a woman behind the wheel.

I can't imagine who would follow us. Just then, the window of the sedan rolls down and I see a familiar face.

Lindsay, Billy's sister. She gives me a wave of her fingers and then the window rolls up again.

"You okay?" Michael asks, not for the first time today.

I whip around to face him.

"I'm fine," I say with a forced smile. I glance at Olivia,

who's engrossed in something happening on the screen of her phone.

I'm grateful for that at this moment.

When I glance back out the window, Lindsay and the sedan are gone. I wonder if I imagined it.

The thought is almost as chilling as the fact that Lindsay was the one following us.

I sit back in my seat again and try to make myself comfortable, knowing that the next few days are going to be anything but.

NINETEEN

OLIVIA KEEPS to herself most of the day, drifting out of her room only to grab snacks. She's like a ghost, haunting the hallways of this house, wordless and expressionless, and completely indifferent to my presence.

I flip through all my streaming services, none of them offering anything that really appeals to me. My mind drifts back to Billy's sister, Lindsay.

How badly she wanted to know about me without coming directly to me at first, following me for the last few days. How hesitant she was. What kind of secret is she keeping about her brother? Is there something about Billy that I don't know?

I go to her contact on my phone a couple of times, wondering if I should bother her. If it would be any help to the ongoing investigation. I would imagine that Underwood already knew about her and he's probably already talked to her.

And the thought of calling Underwood for anything resembling help makes my skin crawl. I'd rather eat glass shards and take my luck with that. He's got it out for me and somehow, I feel like he'd find a way to turn anything around on me. Especially any evidence I present to him.

Not that Lindsay has any evidence. Hell, I don't think she and Billy had talked in years.

And I'm beyond the point of wondering what he was like as a kid. That magic left our relationship a long time ago. I'd rather not put her through the pain of sifting through memories of her estranged brother just for my morbid curiosity. Leave that to that creep Underwood.

Finally, I settle on some reality TV series about housewives from some major metropolitan area far away from Dallas. I watch as they sink their fangs into each other, stirring unnecessary drama and perpetuating the stereotype that women will fight with each other over anything petty.

But it's mindless. And that's what I need right now.

I lose myself in it, focusing only on the storyline before me, forgetting my own. The much more twisty, winding storyline that leads somewhere dark. Somewhere that I haven't been able to pinpoint on a map just yet.

But it goes somewhere. Something exists at the end of this path.

Something I just haven't found yet.

But just as I'm getting nice and deep into the storyline of these purportedly real housewives, my phone buzzes on the end table. I fight my way out of the blanket as it skitters on the glass. I grab it and answer, knowing immediately who it is from the number on the screen.

"This is Kim," I say, my voice clipped. I don't want to bother with niceties with Underwood.

"Nice to talk to you, too, Mrs. Karlsen," he says cooly. I don't like it.

Against my will, it gets under my skin. Underwood has a way of doing that. Most people don't even register on my radar. I have a way of letting things roll right off my back. But there's something about Underwood that gets to me.

Maybe it's his accent. Thick, deep, and southern. Maybe it's because he's like a dog with a bone. The wrong bone, that is. And he's not going to give up on it because he's convinced he's right. That righteousness that he's coming at me with. Maybe that's what irks me.

I conclude that's it before I speak again.

"What can I do for you?" I ask.

"I just wanted to give you an update on things since I was unable to earlier," Underwood says. "We got the toxicology report back on Mr. Karlsen," he goes on.

I sit up straighter on the couch, not sure what to expect, but Underwood's got my attention. That's for sure.

"It seems that your husband was drugged," he says.

"Drugged?" I ask, unable to keep the word from blurting out of my mouth. Somehow, I'm shocked.

I know I shouldn't be. Billy was found face down in the pool with all his clothes on. And even though it was clear that someone had hit him in the face, I was still in some sort of dreamland where maybe he slipped and knocked himself out. But now, with this new piece of information, it's impossible to deny that another person killed Billy.

He really was murdered.

Someone drugged him, and when he was unconscious, they put him into the pool.

"Yes," Underwood says. "Did your husband take anything for sleep?"

"No, nothing," I say.

Billy could fall asleep anywhere. It was me that struggled with insomnia.

"Strange," Underwood says. "It's not everyone that has access to a sleep aid like this. Rohypnol is a very strong drug."

He pauses, making me uncomfortable. I shift in my seat, willing him to say something. I don't care what. *Anything*.

"You sure that he wouldn't have had something like this on hand?" Underwood asks.

The way he poses the question makes me think he's giving me my final out. Like maybe, if Billy had owned strong prescription sleep aids, there might be some possibility in Underwood's mind that all of this had been an accident.

"Of course I'm sure," I tell him, an edge in my voice that I don't intend. "Look," I say, softening my tone. "I'm shocked by all of this. I want to know what happened as much as you do, Detective."

Underwood is silent for a second, his doubt obvious in what I just said.

I can't really blame him. I would be suspicious if the shoe were on the other foot. Still, he has no other evidence other than me being Billy's wife and that, statistically, makes me the most likely to have killed him. I'm beyond frustrated.

"I'm sure you do, Mrs. Karlsen," Underwood says. His voice is cool, even, void of irritation or aggression. Something about it feels dangerous. Worse than if he were yelling at me. Right now, I wish he'd yell at me. It reminds me of one of my mom's boyfriends. One of my almost-step-dads. How he would go silent when he was furious. How I begged him to yell at me once. I begged so hard that he finally slapped me and walked out of the room.

I remain silent even though Underwood can't slap me through the phone.

"I'll be in touch if I need anything else," Underwood says. Then I hear the three beeps letting me know that the call is over. I heave a sigh of relief and sit there in the silence for a moment.

The grandfather clock on the wall nearest the entry hall ticks away. The sound seems louder than usual. Like it could wake the dead in the almost deafening silence throughout the rest of the house.

I sit there for a moment. I'm in shock, I think. Detective Underwood just told me that my husband was drugged. Unless he'd been taking a sleep aid I had no idea about. But Billy *hated* doctors. He'd rather have died than get treatment for anything. Especially anything to do with psychology or sleep. He thought therapy was for hipsters with no kids and a disposable income.

I wonder if his sister would feel the same. Lindsay comes to mind for a moment.

I think about how strange it was to meet her. To see someone who looked so much like Billy. Someone that I'd never met, but should have. I wondered about what went wrong with their family. Not that I'm one to judge. I would have completely separated my life from my mother's if she wasn't dead. I'd never want her in Olivia's life. Especially not now.

A horrible thought occurs to me. That one day Olivia might feel the same about me.

I've done my best to tell her she owes me nothing. I never want her to feel like she has a debt to me the way my mother made me feel about her.

The thoughts going through my mind are overwhelming. I feel my heart beat faster, and I automatically do what I normally do when I'm stressed.

I grab my phone and dial Jackie.

The phone only rings once before she picks up. I can almost smell the scent of her hair through the phone. Cherry and vanilla. Her voice feels like a warm blanket, wrapping me up with the assurance of someone saying, it'll be okay. Whatever it is.

"Hey, you," she says into the receiver. Her voice is quiet.

"Hey," I say. I heave a deep sigh. "Underwood just called me."

"What did he say?" I can practically hear Jackie sit up straighter. Her voice instantly becomes more serious. More alert.

"Apparently, someone drugged Billy or he was taking a really strong sleep aid," I tell her. I lean forward, my elbows on my knees, and I rub my face with my free hand.

"Did you know anything about him being on something like that? What was it?" Jackie asks.

"No. You know how he was. It was Rohypnol, apparently," I tell her.

"He fought going to the doctor. I can't imagine him on something that strong. It's the date rape drug, you know? Or for extreme cases of insomnia. I don't think it's very commonly prescribed," Jackie says.

"Why the hell would he be on that?" I ask, genuinely perplexed, and feeling like I never knew this man.

I'd complained about Billy to her so much that she has a better idea than anyone what our marriage was like, and what things he did that drove me absolutely insane. Like refusing to go to the doctor.

"Yeah," I say. "And he hated psychology and psychiatry. I can't imagine him seeking out a doctor to manage his sleep."

"Me, either," Jackie says.

The pair of us are silent for a moment.

Then Jackie breaks the silence.

"Do you think someone could have given him something?" she probes.

"I guess someone must have," I say. "It's still so hard to imagine."

"There's not really any alternative, Kimmie," she says. Her tone is softer, more understanding.

"I know," I tell her. I know Billy had to have been murdered. It's still so hard to wrap my mind around, though. These people that we thought were our friends, one of them killing him? Billy wasn't the nicest guy, but Christ.

"Did he mention anything about the Blankenships?" Jackie asks.

"No," I say.

"I'm telling you, something weird is going on there," she says. "I think Billy owed them money, Kim."

I roll this over in my mind, not for the first time. I think about Amanda in the super center, picking up those phones.

"I think I'm going to try to find some things out," I tell Jackie.

"Be careful," she says.

"I will," I tell her.

We say goodbye and I stare at my phone, knowing exactly what I'm going to do next.

TWENTY

I DON'T TEXT Jackie to tell her my plans. Michael is another story, though, and ask him if he can come hang out at the house for a little while with Olivia while I run some errands. I don't tell him any more than that. He doesn't need to know more, and he doesn't ask.

I need to know more.

There's a knock at the door and I jump out of my skin in my seat on the couch. I whip around. For a moment, I'm not sure who's at the door. My heart leaps into my throat, then slowly slides back down into its rightful place. I thought it might be Underwood and not Michael.

I compose myself and shake my head, trying to get the constant ghost of Underwood off my back. It should be my dead husband I feel as a companion right now. Not the detective investigating his death. But Underwood haunts me just as well as any ghost. And I think he knows it.

"Who is it?" I ask as I reach for the doorknob.

I see Michael's frame on the other side of the door, still I feel the need to ask. *Just* to make sure, I tell myself. I feel crazy.

Crazier still for what I'm about to do.

"It's me," Michael says, sounding none the wiser about my plans.

I sigh and open the door, gesturing for him to come inside.

"Were you expecting someone else?" he asks.

"No," I say. "Just jumpy."

He looks me over.

"Why are you jumpy?" he asks. His tone is cautious, like he's afraid he might set me off by asking. I try not to bristle at the question. It irritates me, though. Makes me feel like Michael thinks I'm not handling this very well. Which, anyone could argue, I'm not. But I'm doing my best. Who the hell would know the correct way to handle such a situation?

"I don't know," I tell him with a pressed smile. "Sit."

Michael looks at me skeptically.

"Olivia's in her room. Probably playing video games. You can drag her out of there if you want, or you can go play with her. Or y'all can play in here," I tell him.

"I'm not a babysitter, Kim. I don't need instructions," he says, eying me with the same skepticism. He detects that I'm up to something. "Where are you going tonight?"

"I told you, I need to run some errands," I say, looking away.

I've never been the best liar. I remember getting my ass beat over the fact when I was a kid. Never by my mom, but always by one of her boyfriends. She never stopped it, either. I half-expect Michael to bend me over and smack my ass. Not in a sexy way. In a brutal way.

"What errands do you need to run at nine at night?" he asks. "Come on, you can talk to me."

"I just need to pick up a prescription," I tell him, lying on the spot, coming up with the first thing I can. Thinking about Billy being drugged brings it to mind. I wonder if I'll regret that later.

Michael looks suspicious, but drops it. And I'm thankful for that.

"I'll be back soon," I tell him. "The pharmacy is across town."

I try to buy myself some time.

"Across town?" Michael asks.

I shoot him a look that dares him to ask another question. He throws his hands up in mock surrender and sits down on the couch, reaching for the remote on the end table. For a moment, it almost feels like we're married again. Me running to the store to grab something that Olivia needs. Diapers, rash cream. Michael wanting to stay with her because he knew it would stress me out. Even as a baby, I couldn't soothe her the way he could.

I stare at him for a moment, hovering in the doorway and putting off the task in front of me.

But then I slip out the door and lock it on my way out, heading out into the night.

Heading to Billy's office.

I PULL INTO THE LOT. Billy's office is in a series of new office buildings that look more like a fancy neighborhood than anything. I know it's already been searched, but I have to see for myself. The only thing giving it away is that each of them has a bronze plaque featuring the names of the businesses they house.

There's one street lamp on the corner of the property and another at the end of the parking lot, casting the spaces in front of the building in shadow. I pull in to one of them and stare at the black glass of the double doors that lead into the office space.

Billy's office is in the back of the building. He shares the building with a therapist and a lawyer. Three offices in one large floor plan, all of them small enough to feel welcoming but clearly profitable enough to be in a new space on a prized bit of commercial real estate. I used to joke that the lawyer and the therapist were there to deal with things when the investments went wrong.

The joke suddenly isn't that funny anymore. Not sitting here in the dark, waiting to work up the courage to go in there and see if I can find anything that might point me in the right direction. Or might help me point Underwood in the right direction. Not that I think he'll do much listening to me.

I feel like the whole thing is on my shoulders. I need to go to Underwood with something irrefutable. And maybe that something is hidden inside Billy's office.

I kill the engine and steel my resolve. I slip out and head for the door.

I never had a key to Billy's office. It always struck me

as annoying, but not that strange. I had to get the only one he had out of his car after he died. I figured there were a lot of privacy laws about who could see what's inside a financial investor's office. It was the nosy wife in me that wanted to come and go as I pleased.

Or maybe it wasn't nosiness.

Maybe it was gut instinct.

The thought makes my stomach drop as I slide the key into the lock and open the door. I quickly shut it and lock it behind me, saying a silent prayer that no cops see my car outside. Not that I'm really breaking the law or anything. I just know how it'll look to Underwood. They already did their searches. Even as we speak, they're analyzing the contents of his computer.

And God, will he run with whatever they find.

I inhale sharply as I head down a hallway lit only by the dim red of an exit sign, pointing me toward the side of the building where, presumably, I'd be able to escape from a fire. I try to slow my heart down, taking deep breaths, inhaling and exhaling like I'm in a birthing class. It does little to help. By the time I reach the frosted glass and cherry wood door that has a plaque next to it with Billy's name on it, my heart is racing and I'm sweating under my arms even though it's cold as an ice cube in this place.

My palm is sweaty as I put the key into the doorknob, slide it to, and crank it clockwise in my slightly slippery grip.

The door yawns open with a creak, its brand new hinges a little too tight. The sound makes me cringe, feeling like someone out on the street could hear it. Like someone might be out there listening for just such a sound. I relax my face and open my eyes to darkness.

I reach for the switch and flip it on, bathing the place in bright light that makes my pupils contract quickly and sends a shooting pain through my head. I blink as I adjust my eyes.

The silence in the building is heavy, almost tangible, and I feel like every movement I make cuts through it, making incredible noise.

I swallow, my mouth dry, and walk past Jackie's desk. I head to the door that leads into Billy's office and go inside, flipping on another light switch.

His desk is huge. The kind of executive desk you see at really expensive furniture stores. In fact, there's not a piece of furniture in here that doesn't look like money. Just like our house. I think again about the Blankenships. Even if Billy owed them money, he'd be good for it. They'd have no reason to do anything to him. How would they get their money if they did?

Still, I have a lot of questions.

Bookshelves line the walls, none of them housing any fiction. Billy didn't read. These were purely for business binders and financial magazines. Oh, and awards and certifications that he proudly displayed to his clients. I couldn't fault him for that. I would do the same. It was good for business. It instilled confidence in his clients.

I walk around and sit in the gargantuan chair. The leather is soft against my exposed legs. Cold, too. I stare at the computer in front of me.

Jackie found the note on his desk, didn't she?

It's pristine, though. There isn't a hoard of sticky notes, littering the space chaotically. Everything's in order.

I decide to look in the desk instead of worrying about what's on top. If the sticky note was handwritten, there might be other pieces of handwritten evidence of...what? I'm not sure. Something. Something the cops missed.

I open the top center drawer, and just as I suspected, the whole thing is meticulously organized. I can practically hear Billy groaning and bitching at Olivia when she'd leave things in a mess behind her, a perpetual teenage tornado. It was one of the few things he ever got upset with her about.

The drawer reflects that. His insistence on tidiness. He wanted the house to look a certain way all the time. He was the one who insisted on hiring cleaners when I couldn't keep up with the amount of square footage he'd said we needed.

I reach into the drawer and pick up a pen with his name on it, printed on the barrel of the metal. It's one of those pens that businesses give to clients, presumably hoping the client will use it and the business will always remain top of mind for whatever services they provide. I wonder how many people have these pens.

I wonder if Dan and Amanda have one.

The thought creeps in, unbidden. I keep rifling through the desk, trying to put things back where they go as I search through them.

But when I get to the filing drawer, it's empty. The cops took everything. *Shit.*

Defeated, I come to the bottom right drawer and pull it open. The wood groans as I do, almost like it doesn't quite fit in the space allotted for it. Like maybe the wood has warped and expanded, making it hard to slide back into the little hole.

I pull it all the way out and see nothing out of the ordinary. Papers, labels, paperclips. Stuff like that. But as I pull it a little bit further, something happens.

A piece of wood at the back of the drawer cracks down the middle. The back of the drawer itself. I tug it out further, horrified by the noise it made. I wonder if I'm going to be able to get it back in.

But when I get it out, I notice something else.

The little crack splinters the wood and makes the back of the drawer pop inward. But when I tug on it, I realize that it's not the back of the drawer.

There's a hidden space behind it.

My heart beats faster.

I tug it a little further, breaking it at the place where it's cracked. It comes loose, apparently broken there once before.

And then a wad comes pushing out of it, obviously too big for the little space it's been allocated to. Pieces of thick paper, curved into a roll, several of them on top of each other. But when one of them unrolls, I realize what they are.

Printed photos.

The corner of one picture comes into view. I reach for them, pulling them out of the false back to the drawer. There are a lot. After I pull out one rolled up wad of them, I reach further inside and pull out another. There are likely thirty photographs.

And then I turn them over.

The pictures are of a woman's body. Her face isn't in any of the shots. They're sexual in nature. In one of them, I see one of Billy's shoes. Something that wouldn't seem like a big deal considering that I've never been monogamous. But this is a *betrayal*.

This is behind my back.

This is a secret that Billy clearly didn't want anyone to know about.

After he'd told me that he'd only be happy if we were monogamous.

He had photographs of a naked woman in his desk at the office the whole time.

How old were they? There was no way to tell.

The pictures look like they were taken in a hotel room. The walls are off-white. The carpet is berber, nondescript beige. It looks like it could have been taken at any hotel in the area. There's nothing that gives me an idea of which one.

But I know it's not our house, and it's not a house I recognize.

Whoever this was, Billy was with her, alone. And I knew nothing about it.

I'm not hurt that he slept with someone else. I would have been happy for him to do that. I'm upset that this was a secret. Especially when he'd acted like he was so above the idea of ethical non-monogamy. Personally offended by it.

I guess he was only interested in the unethical kind.

I notice that my hand is shaking the picture in my hand like a leaf rattling in the wind. I drop it on the desk next to the others.

And then a thought occurs to me.

What if this woman was married?

And what if her husband killed Billy?

TWENTY-ONE

THE THOUGHT SPLASHES over me like a bucket of cold water emptied right above my head. It stings. Shock rolls through me. I know I came here looking for something substantial. Could this be it?

I reach for my cell phone, intending to call Underwood.

I hesitate.

What will he think about me being at Billy's office this late? Or at all? Up here by myself in the dark? I don't think it would make him feel more sympathetic to me. That's for sure.

Never in my life have I cared this much what a man thinks. Turns out when the man is bent on prosecuting me for a crime I didn't commit, I'm a lot more invested in that man's thoughts. It's irritating and nothing like me. I hate how I feel: controlled by Underwood. Under his thumb. Like he's watching me all the time, waiting for me in a dark alley or around a corner.

I'm sure that's exactly how he wants it to feel for me.

I wonder where he is right now. If he's stewing over this case, looking for a way to pin it on me.

He's probably not. Maybe he has a life. I know he has a soon-to-be ex-wife. Friends, family, hobbies. Maybe he's at the bowling alley with his league tonight. The idea makes a bitter laugh bubble up in my chest. The thought of Underwood doing anything for fun is hard to imagine. I bet his idea of fun is what he's doing to me right now.

The laugh quickly fades at the thought.

I take a deep breath, inhaling slowly through my nose, breathing out through my mouth. It reminds me of a yoga class I used to go to. Somehow, I don't think yoga was designed for calming you down right after your husband's been murdered.

The breathing exercise does nothing to calm me. I grab the photographs and sweep them into my bag, pulling it up on my shoulder and kicking the desk drawer shut at my feet. I stand up, walk over and turn the light off, and head back out of Billy's office. I lock the doors behind me and get into the car.

It's only then that I feel I can relax. I check twice to make sure no one's in the back waiting for me. I turn around and start the engine, relaxing against the headrest for a moment.

Billy was having an affair. That much is clear.

Who was he having an affair with?

I speed back to the house, having to remind myself over and over to slow down. The last thing I want is a ticket at midnight. That'll look good on my record considering all of this.

I pull into the driveway and into the garage. The

neighborhood is fast asleep. Michael's truck is still in the driveway, of course. When I come in, I try not to make too much noise. I leave my bag in the laundry room and then emerge into the kitchen. I spot the top of his head over the counter, still sitting on the couch. The television is blaring, and I hear Michael snoring. Olivia is nowhere to be found, and I assume she went to bed. Michael has one of the twenty-four-hour cable news networks playing as his lullaby.

I reach for the remote and switch it off, then gently jiggle his arm.

"Hey," I whisper.

Michael's eyes slowly open. He's not startled, but for a moment he looks confused. Maybe like he's unsure of where he is or even who I am. But then recognition registers on his features and a wide smile breaks across his face.

"You're back. What time is it?" he croaks.

"Past midnight," I say. "You can stay here."

Michael looks exhausted. I feel bad for him to leave in the middle of the night. But he says nothing, only sitting up straight on the couch and bringing his feet down to the floor, off the coffee table.

"I'll get going," he murmurs, rubbing his face.

"Just stay," I tell him. I run to the linen cabinet and grab him a blanket. An over-sized one. I spread it over him and encourage him to lie down on the couch. I tuck him in and he's just sleepy enough that he lets me.

"Goodnight," I tell him.

And before I'm even out of the room, I hear him snore again, a comfort to me tonight.

I walk down the hallway that leads to Olivia's room. I turn the doorknob and peek inside. She's snoring, too. It sounds just like Michael, but not nearly as loud or aggressive. The thought makes me smile. As soon as I shut her door, though, I'm reminded of what's waiting for me in the laundry room.

I grab my bag and then swipe my laptop off the bar counter. I head into my bedroom and close the door, finding myself making sure that I do so silently. I grimace when it makes a slight knocking noise as I let go of the doorknob.

The room is far too quiet.

"Just relax," I tell myself.

I crawl into bed with my laptop and my bag. I fish the photographs out and I spread them over my comforter.

I look at them as a whole. All the same woman, as far as I can tell. In every image, she's wearing the same anklet. It's delicate, a thin chain with a single charm. Tiny and almost blurred in the photos. It's a horseshoe.

I check the other pictures, making sure I'm seeing what I think I'm seeing. I wonder if they were all taken at the same time. The girl's toenails are red in every picture. Either she always gets the same color for her pedicures or it was the same time and clearly the same place.

Could she have been a sex worker?

Would Billy have called someone for that?

I know we weren't sleeping together at the end. Could it have driven him to calling a professional? Why didn't he just talk to me?

Would it have mattered if he had?

The last question hits me like a ton of bricks. I wanted out of my marriage so bad.

And I got my wish. Billy's gone. *For good.*

There's just the little matter of me being a suspect, even though they haven't formally stated that. Divorce would have been easier. No matter how messy it got, it could never be like things are now.

I mentally kick myself for not having the strength to end it when I knew I should have.

I stayed with him when I knew it was over.

The stability Billy provided us with was what kept me. His income kept Olivia in a private school. It kept her participating in sports. It gave her whatever she needed or even wanted. I might have left him if it hadn't been for her. So I don't regret the way things went.

I would do anything to make Olivia's life easier.

I sigh, looking at the photographs, wondering who my husband really was.

Do we ever really know anyone?

I feel like we're all keeping secrets. Each of us has that one thing—that one experience, that one thing you did or said, that one part of your life—that we'll go to our graves with. Everyone has that, I think.

Or maybe it's just people like me and Billy.

Bad people.

The anklet catches my eye again. It sparks a memory. It's flitting, not entirely whole. Just a vision of something. Someone wearing it. I can't put my finger on it.

My brain switches into overdrive, combing through every available memory, looking for that horseshoe charm. I try to remember where I've seen it. Why it looks familiar.

It's right there, buried somewhere in my brain. I know I've seen this before. I know I can identify the person wearing it. I know this.

Still, the name and image of the woman's face won't come to me.

Maybe I'm kidding myself.

I open my laptop, sick of thinking about it. I tell myself to drop it. Stewing over that all night is just going to give me an ulcer. And there's a chance that the answer I'm seeking will come to me overnight. Maybe I'll wake up with a clear memory of where I've seen the damned anklet before.

I log in to Facebook and start scrolling mindlessly. I turn on the television for background noise and I pack up the photographs back into my bag. I sift through posts made by friends, family, and acquaintances. The last two categories practically being one and the same.

In the middle of my scrolling, a little red notification pops up on the bell in the upper right-hand corner of the screen. I click on it and see that I've got a friend request.

Lindsay Karlsen.

Billy's sister.

I click on her profile.

There's nothing remarkable about it. It's sparse. I imagine she has it set to private, sharing as little as possible with the outside world. Until the night of the visitation, I didn't know Lindsay even existed. This entire part of Billy's life that he hadn't shared with me.

Suddenly, the cheating doesn't seem that strange.

Maybe he always kept his life compartmentalized, and I just had no idea how good he was at it.

It's a less chilling thought than the idea that I've been living with a stranger all these years.

I accept Lindsay's friend request and navigate back to the main feed.

A picture of Nicole and Jason pops up. The two of them out on a date night. One picture taken by Nicole and the other taken by Jason. Both of them sitting at a booth at a Chili's. They don't go out to eat often. Both of them on a teacher's salary and both of them being financially conscious all the time. I wouldn't be surprised if they had a better nest egg than any of the rest of us. They're always smart with money. I imagine it's a special occasion.

Sure enough, I read the caption, and it's Jason's birthday.

Normally, I'd be embarrassed that I didn't remember it. I'd shoot Nicole a message to the group chat that we girls shared. Tell her to wish Jason a happy birthday for me and tell her I hope they had fun tonight.

But everything is different.

The group chat has been minimal since Billy died. Nicole checked on me after the funeral. Amanda was notably absent from the messages that followed Nicole's. I can't really blame her after the scene I made.

I don't feel comfortable just sending her a text out of nowhere. It feels like I'm stalking them. Would it make her think I suspect them of something?

It would feel weird. For both of us.

With a little of sadness, I leave it as a scab

unscratched. Better for all of us that way. No blood. No scar. No messiness.

I stare at the pictures of the two of them for a moment longer, though. And it leads me to click on Nicole's profile. They're so happy with each other it's almost sickening. The two of them are so in love even now. They act like newlyweds. They always have. Ever since I've known them.

I scroll through old pictures and posts. Times they've gone to events. Stuff for the school. Nicole won teacher of the year last year. Jason won it the year before. Both of them are active within the PTSA even though they don't have kids. They both care about education and the future for the kids they teach.

From the outside looking in, their lives are perfect.

And no one likely even knows that they were there the night that Billy died.

Was murdered.

It makes me feel so alone.

I think about calling Jackie, and then I remember it's close to one in the morning. I sigh and lay the phone down and go back to scrolling Nicole's old photos and posts.

And then I find one that I remember.

When they went on that cruise her mom gave them for an anniversary gift.

Nicole posted all about it. Pictures of the two of them exploring little islands in the Caribbean. The entertainment on the ship. Meals. Shopping. All of it. I expand the post, looking at all of the pictures.

I see one of them at a fancy dinner.

Then I see one of them shopping in one of the ports.

A bag from a jewelry store.

Then I see something that stops the world from spinning around me.

Nicole. Her feet next to her husband's.

Perfectly manicured toes in the sand. And around her ankle is a silver chain bearing a horseshoe charm.

TWENTY-TWO

I WAIT until 7:27 the next morning to call Jackie. I call her before I even get out of bed. She answers on the first ring.

"What's up, Kimmie?" she asks on the other end of the phone, sounding chipper.

"Come over. Now."

"Well, good morning to you, too," she says.

"Sorry," I say. "Just come over. Please," I say.

"I'm on my way," she says. Then she hangs up the phone.

I stare at mine for a moment and then jump off the bed, remembering that I have an ex-husband sleeping on my couch. In just my sleep shorts and a muscle tank, I rush to the living room, ready to shout for Michael to get up.

But when I get there, he's gone.

I open my mouth to say his name before it fully registers. The blanket is folded neatly on the couch and there's a note on top of it. I grab it.

Thanks for the accommodations
Michael

It sends a shooting pain through my chest. An unexpected reaction.

Michael used to leave notes all over the house for me when we were married. Especially when we had first married. Anytime he had to leave when I was asleep, he was sure to leave me at least one note. Many times multiple notes.

I hold it in my fingers and run my thumb over his handwriting.

Had things been simpler then?

I think about how much Michael had wanted to keep us together, even after I told him that I didn't want to be monogamous. I couldn't stand the idea of living that lifestyle when he wouldn't be a part of it. Michael would have let me do whatever I wanted and I couldn't do that to him. I had to leave.

Maybe things hadn't been that simple. Maybe it's the rose tint on the rearview mirror.

Still, I can't bring myself to trash the note. I tuck it into my wallet, behind my cash.

I brew some coffee, though I'm hardly in need of caffeine to be awake. I couldn't have slept after seeing that picture of Nicole's feet in the sand. I don't think anyone in my position could have. I saw the anklet. It's there in those photographs and there in that picture on Facebook.

My husband and one of my closest friends were having an affair.

I drum my fingers on the counter and rest my chin in

my hand, looking out the window when I see Jackie pulling into the drive. I meet her at the door and instantly wrap her in a hug.

"Whoa," she laughs. "What's that for?"

She hugs me back, though. A hand rubbing gentle circles on my back.

"It's a long story," I breathe, inhaling the scent of her. I pull away and look at her. Even now, wearing sweats and a crop top, her hair pulled up in a bandana, she's gorgeous. I don't think Jackie is ever not gorgeous.

"Well, let me come in so you can tell me," she says.

She squeezes my hand and passes by me into the house. I close the door behind us, finding myself checking the lock twice before I turn to head into the kitchen. I grab us both a cup of coffee and invite her out onto the back patio. Olivia's still asleep and the last thing I want is for her to wake up while we're talking about all of this.

I close the door behind us, and we sit down at the metal table under the pergola. The sun isn't over the house yet and it's pleasant out here still. There's a little breeze that I only notice because it cools my underarms as I step outside. I'm sweating. I'm nervous.

"So, what's going on?" Jackie asks. She leans forward onto the table.

I dart to the bedroom and grab the tote with my laptop and the photos. I go back outside and slide it onto the table. I pull out the photographs and the laptop.

"I found these in Billy's desk last night," I tell her, spreading them across the table.

Jackie takes off her sunglasses.

I glance at them. They look just like my Jackie O's.

My eyes linger on them for a moment as I wonder where I put mine. I haven't seen them since the funeral. Oh, well. I don't need them right now. I focus on the pictures.

"Where did you find these?" Jackie asks.

"Behind a false back in one of the drawers," I say. "I guess he hid them there."

Jackie pores over the photos, taking each one individually and inspecting it as much as I had last night. She says nothing for a long time.

"He was cheating on me," I tell her.

Jackie places the photograph she's holding back on the table. All of them are arranged in rows of six. Five of them. Anyone looking from over the fence might think I was meeting with a home decorator about a makeover, each shot a potential piece of decor going into the house.

I wish that's what we were discussing.

"With who?" Jackie asks softly. She looks up at me, searching my face. I wonder if she thinks I've lost it.

"Well, I started going through Facebook pictures last night. And something got me on Nicole's page. I ended up on a post from when they went on that cruise her mom gave them. You remember that?"

"Yeah," Jackie says.

"Well, there was a picture of them with a bag from a jewelry store in the Caribbean. Then there was a picture with this same anklet on Nicole's foot," I say, popping my laptop open. I turn it around for Jackie, not having navigated off the page last night in fear that it might disappear on me.

Jackie stares at it for a moment.

"I can't believe this," she says.

"I can't either," I tell her. "But do you know what this means?" I ask.

Realization dawns on Jackie's face.

"You don't think…"

"I do," I say. "I think maybe Jason had something to do with all of this. What if he found out and settled up with Billy, man-to-man?"

Jackie looks at me, then back at the screen, then back to me.

"Do you think Jason is capable of that?" she asks.

"I don't know, Jackie," I say. "I'm willing to believe just about anything at this point. I don't think we ever really know anyone. I didn't know my own husband. How could I have known hers?"

Jackie is silent for a moment.

"I thought about calling Underwood last night and talked myself out of it," I tell her.

"Really? Why didn't you call him?"

"I couldn't imagine that me going to Billy's office after midnight and finding pictures of another woman in his desk would register with Underwood as anything but shady. They searched the office. Why wouldn't they have found them? He might think I planted them there. I couldn't make up my mind, so I didn't call him. But now, I think I should. Don't you?"

"I don't know," Jackie says. "What can they really tell from them? They're photographs. There's not metadata," she says.

I think about that for a moment. She's right. They won't be able to tell more than I have.

"But I can show them the picture of the anklet," I tell her.

"Are you sure you want to do that? Look, I'm just looking out for you. You've gotta think about what he'll do with this information. He might find a way to use it against you. Think you planted it, like you said," she goes on. "I think maybe you should just destroy them."

I roll this over in my mind.

Jackie doesn't stay much longer. I hug her before she leaves and find myself wishing she'd stay. Wishing that she didn't have Nathan to run home to. I want her to be here with me all day. I say goodbye to her, anyway.

After she leaves, I go back out to the patio, and I look at the photos.

I go over them each and every one for the millionth time.

I have no way of knowing exactly how Underwood is going to perceive this, but it's the best lead I've gotten this whole time. It's the best shot I'm probably going to get at figuring out who killed my husband.

So I pick up the phone and dial.

TWENTY-THREE

IT'S 9:13 when Underwood rolls up in the driveway. Olivia is in her room. I brought her breakfast in bed and instructed her to stay there until I came and got her. She'd given me a strange look, but Olivia would do as I said. It's one of the few things in my life that I can count on right now.

I wait by the door until I see his frame darken the entry hall. Hesitating, I don't open the door until he rings the doorbell. I swing it slowly, trying not to seem nervous. I hate myself instantly when I involuntarily flash him a smile. I'm not sure I've ever smiled at him.

He returns it, but the expression looks strange on his face. Like he's wearing a mask.

I wonder if there's anything that makes him laugh. Does he laugh at all? Can he?

The thought makes me giggle.

Our eyes meet and I clear my throat.

"To what do I owe the pleasure of this visit, Mrs.

Karlsen?" His southern accent hugs each word, making one flow smoothly into the next like a verse out of a poem and not a question out of a detective's mouth.

"I found something," I tell him, taking no time for niceties. It's best to get it over with, however Underwood is going to receive this.

Underwood arches an eyebrow, waiting for me to continue.

"Pictures. At Billy's office," I say.

"We searched your husband's office," Underwood says. There's a hint of defensiveness in his voice. Like I'm accusing him of not doing his job. And that's something I'm sure he'll take extremely personally.

"They were hidden in the back of a drawer. There was a false back to it. These were behind it," I say, handing him the stack of pictures.

Underwood goes through them one by one, looking at each with detached interest.

My breathing grows shallow as he does so. I'm almost certain he can hear it.

"Who is this woman?" Underwood asks.

"Well," I say. "I think it's Nicole Phelps."

"From the night of the murder."

It's more like he's talking to himself than to me. I say nothing. He goes through some more of the pictures.

"I think they were having an affair," I say to Underwood.

The words come out softly, almost like I'm afraid to speak them. Afraid of the reality they might imply. Not just of the infidelity, but of what it could mean about that night and who drugged Billy and put him in the pool.

"Awfully convenient to find them now. Did you have any suspicions of their affair?" Underwood asks, looking up at me.

"None," I tell him, trying to ignore the implication. I was afraid of this.

"Most women have some sort of intuition about their husbands having affairs. Are you sure there wasn't anything that might have led you to believe that before you found these?" The way he says it is pointed, like he's getting at something else. And my heart sinks.

I steel myself, feeling where this is going.

"I had no clue that he might've been having an affair," I say. "But I'm not sure how well I knew him at all. I met his sister for the first time at his visitation." I try to stay calm as I speak but I feel anger bubbling inside of me.

Underwood looks taken aback at this.

"I was unaware he had a sister. You hadn't met her before?" he asks.

"Never," I tell him.

He looks at the pictures and then back at me.

"You told me you guys weren't having any problems," he says. "Was communication a problem?"

"In that we just…didn't?" I ask. "I guess you could say so, looking back in hindsight."

"Fair enough," Underwood says.

"I thought I knew him, though," I say. It's the most vulnerable I've been with Underwood.

He listens without speaking.

"I didn't realize you could live every day with someone and still not know them, I guess," I tell him. I look up and meet his eyes. If I didn't know any better, I'd swear I see compassion there.

He clears his throat and speaks.

"I was married once upon a time," he says. "We got married when we were kids. Right out of high school. I became a cop. She became a teacher. Then I got serious about becoming a detective. And I became a detective. And then it was like I was married to the force and my wife was my mistress without any of the excitement. I should have seen it coming a mile away. She had an affair, and she left me before I even noticed she was running around."

"I'm sorry," I tell him.

"Don't be," he says. "It's just to say that yes, you can live with someone for years and not know when they step out of the confines of your marriage. It's very possible. And it's possible to not really know someone at all when you think, beyond a shadow of a doubt, that you know them better than anyone."

I stand there in silence, shocked at Underwood's confession. It's more words than he's spoken to me in a single conversation since I met him. I hesitate to respond, appreciating his vulnerability.

"I guess it can happen to anyone," I finally say, hoping it's the right choice.

He looks up at me and cracks a smile. This time, it doesn't seem awkward. This time, it seems genuine.

"I guess there is one other thing that might be relevant when it comes to Nicole and my husband," I tell him. I feel a surge of nausea, needing to get out the words hovering in my throat. I've avoided telling him this since the beginning. I urged everyone to keep quiet, thinking it was better for everyone. But maybe I should have been totally transparent from the beginning.

"What's that?" Underwood asks.

"We live a different lifestyle, I guess you could say," I tell him.

He arches an eyebrow. Not for the first time.

"And my husband had slept with Nicole before," I say.

"So, he cheated on you with her once before?" he tries to clarify.

"No," I say. "Not cheated."

Underwood looks at me, searching my face for what I mean.

"We had an open relationship," I tell him. "Sort of."

"So, it was okay that he slept with Nicole?" Underwood asks, confused.

"That time, yes. Because I knew about it. It wasn't a secret," I tell him. "There's a difference between agreeing on the rules of the game and playing another game behind your partner's back."

Underwood nods.

"We were swingers," I add.

He nods again, understanding.

"That had to be difficult for you to tell me," he says. "One of my officers had that suspicion," he adds.

I blush, horrified, suddenly worrying about what they said between them. What they thought of us before they even knew our names. What judgments they must have made. I've heard it all before, none of it kind or flattering.

"Well, there it is," I say.

"So, you think your husband might have wanted to take this behind your back then?" he asks.

"He had to have. It's Nicole in those photos," I tell him. "They were hidden in his desk and," I hesitate. "And he had stopped participating in...lifestyle stuff."

"Makes sense. Why would he need to at that point?" Underwood asks to no one in particular.

"Right?" I say. I feel relief that he's coming to the same conclusions I did.

"But how do you know this is Nicole?" he asks.

I bring out my laptop and open it, the screen the same as earlier.

"This is an anklet Nicole got on vacation a few years ago. I knew I recognized it. And here it is," I point at the screen.

"Very interesting," Underwood says. "And you had no idea about any of this until now?"

"No idea," I confirm.

Underwood nods, seeming to roll this over in his mind.

"I'm going to take these with me back to the station," he says, waving one of the photographs.

"Take all of them," I say.

"And send me a link to that post," he adds. "Screenshot it now, in case it goes missing."

I nod, intent on doing exactly as he says.

He turns to walk to the door. He opens it and I step outside behind him.

"Detective," I say.

He turns and looks at me.

"Hmm?"
"Thank you."

TWENTY-FOUR

THAT AFTERNOON, I come into the living room and Olivia is spread out on the couch. Her laptop on one side of her, her phone on the other, a gaming headset hanging on her neck and a controller in her hand. The sight makes me smile and calls back to a more normal time in our lives. It gives me the hope that we might return there. Or to some semblance of it. Kids really are as resilient as the experts say they are. That's what a therapist told Michael and I when we asked for advice about breaking the news of our divorce to her.

I sigh and pick up her phone, moving it to the end table and putting the pillow back against the armrest. I take a seat on the couch next to her.

"When is it my turn?" I ask.

Olivia rolls her eyes, but she laughs a little bit.

"You'd die immediately," she tells me.

She's not wrong. In the few times I have tried to play with her and her dad, I've failed miserably.

"I wanted to talk to you about something," I tell her.

She doesn't bother to look away from the game.

"I'm listening."

"I'd like your full attention, please," I say.

Olivia grudgingly pauses the game and looks at me, the controller still in her hand, a reminder that she doesn't have all day for me.

"Are you ready to go back to school?" I ask, knowing I need to cut right to the chase with her.

It's something about her that I appreciate. It's also something that sometimes gets under my skin, mostly because I can be the same way. Olivia and I both generally have no time for pleasantries or sugar coating things.

"Yeah," Olivia says. "Is that what you wanted to talk to me about?" She gives me a look that tells me she thinks I've lost my mind to consider this an important topic of conversation.

"Okay then," I say with a chuckle. "I just wanted to be sure you're ready."

She turns her game back on.

"I've been ready," she says as she blasts some alien creature into oblivion.

I'M grocery shopping when I get the phone call.

"Mrs. Karlsen?" An older woman speaks through the phone. I don't recognize the voice instantly. My stomach drops. I know it can't be good, given the circumstances I've been in.

"This is she," I say.

"I'm calling about your daughter, Olivia Williams," she says.

"What's wrong?" I ask. "Is she okay?"

"She's fine." The woman on the other end of the line is quick to assure me, but it does nothing to ease my anxiety.

"What happened?" I ask.

"Well, Olivia got into a fight at school today," she says.

"She what?"

"She and another student were caught fighting in the bathroom. Olivia split the other girl's lip and EMTs had to be called. She's currently getting stitched up at the hospital," she says.

The grocery store bends around me, my vision starting to tunnel. Never in her life has Olivia been in trouble like this at school. She's never even had so much as a note in her folder telling me that she's been any kind of problem in class.

"Well, what happened?" I ask. "Did the other girl start it?"

"It seems that Olivia reacted to something she said," the woman tells me.

I'm speechless for a moment.

Olivia has never been the kind of kid to solve a problem at school with violence. She's never been a bully. All I can imagine is that this woman doesn't have the full story and Olivia had a reason to defend herself.

"I'll be there in five minutes," I say.

I hang up the phone and walk away from my cart, leaving it standing in the aisle next to the breakfast cereal.

I speed all the way to Olivia's school. I pull up outside the main building and park in the no-parking zone, not caring if I'm breaking the rules or a law. I jog into the building and go straight to the office.

A woman looks up at me from the receptionist's desk.

"I'm Olivia Williams's mother," I say. "Something happened with her today."

"Oh, yeah. Hang on just a second," the woman says. It's so casual, like she sees this sort of thing every day. She makes a quick phone call and then steps out from behind the desk and leads me down the hall to an office. She opens the door and I see Olivia sitting at a table. It looks like an interrogation room at the police station. I rush over to her side.

"What happened?" I ask, taking her face in my hands.

She shrugs away from me.

"Don't touch me," she says.

Her words drip with venom.

Olivia has never talked to me like that. It's like a punch to the gut. I stand back up.

"What happened today, Olivia?" I ask more sternly.

"I got into a fight," she says, and leaves it at that.

"Were you defending yourself?" I ask.

"Not exactly," she says. "More like I was defending you."

"Oh, my God," I whisper, bringing a hand to my mouth. One of the kids probably called me a murderer. Insinuated me as my husband's killer in some way. And Olivia was bearing the brunt of that. The realization is like being dunked into a tank of cold water at the fair after someone finally lands a pitch on the rusty target. "Olivia, I'm so sorry."

She doesn't say anything and she won't make eye contact with me.

I don't know what to say to her.

Someone opens the door behind us and comes into the room. I instantly recognize the woman. Olivia's guidance counselor. I've met with her before. Never over something serious. We worked together on a PTSA project last year.

"Mrs. Karlsen," she says. "I'm glad you're here."

I sigh and look back at Olivia. She doesn't even acknowledge that her counselor is in the room. I'm struck by the sudden urge to snap at her, make her behave. But the counselor speaks before I can.

"Olivia," she says. "Why don't you go and wait outside the office for a little while so I can talk to your mom?"

Olivia gets up without a word and disappears out the door without so much as a glance back at me.

"Is this about what happened to her step-dad?" I ask.

"Mrs. Karlsen—"

"Was someone teasing her about his death?"

"This isn't about your husband," she says.

I stop short in my rapid-fire questions.

"What's it about then?" I ask.

"It's about you," she says.

I inhale sharply, feeling like I've been slapped. Brought back to reality.

"Me?" I ask with an incredulous laugh.

"It seems that there are some rumors swirling around with the students," she says gingerly.

"What kind of rumors?" I say, dread knotting in my gut.

"The girls are whispering about the night of your husband's death. Saying that there was some sort of unsavory party going on at your house. All nonsense, I'm sure," she says, looking pointedly at me. "The rumor is that you were having some sort of sex party at your house. The kids are using the words 'swingers' party'."

I feel the blood drain out of my face.

My pulse thunders in my ears.

My vision tunnels and everything sounds like static. I can't feel my legs, but I try to stand. Try to run from the room. Try to run to Olivia.

Olivia.

"I am so sorry to have to be the one to tell you this," she says.

I gasp and find myself hyperventilating.

Olivia doesn't know about that. Olivia was never going to know about it. Olivia was always protected. I always kept her safe from that.

I catch my breath and look at Olivia's counselor.

"And someone said this to Olivia?" I ask, my voice barely a whisper.

"Yes," the guidance counselor says.

"And Olivia didn't react well?"

"To say the least," she says. "I don't blame her for being upset," she adds. "No one wants to hear someone talk about their family like that."

I almost laugh.

I want to tell her, but it's all true! Doesn't that make it even worse?

I feel myself on the verge of tears.

"I know Olivia is a good kid," she says, reaching for my hand on the table. She takes it in hers. It makes it worse and I feel a tear sneak over my eyelid, landing hot on my collarbone. "Just have a talk with her. I'm going to see the girl's parents this afternoon as well."

"Can I ask who it was?"

"The girl's name is Hillary," she says. "Hillary Underwood."

TWENTY-FIVE

OLIVIA REFUSES to ride in the passenger seat. She climbs into the back, making a dramatic showing of slamming the door. She puts on her seatbelt and crosses her arms, looking mournfully out the window. Olivia's in anguish and it's all my fault.

I watch her in the rearview as we head across town. I steal glances at every stoplight, trying to gather the courage to say her name. To see if she'll even look in my direction.

If I was her, I wouldn't want to look at me ever again.

The thought blasts a hollow ache through me. Like my chest is a coal mine, and the notion is dynamite, clearing a path for the emptiness that fills it.

I need to talk to Michael. I have to tell him.

I'm dreading it. I don't know exactly how he'll react.

"Olivia," I venture, glancing into the rearview but looking away before she has any chance to turn her head.

She says nothing in return.

I swallow, my mouth cotton and my tongue dry as the

Texas panhandle in a drought. My throat scratches and I clear it, but it does little good. I feel nauseous. This is the last conversation I wanted to be having with my daughter. Today or *ever*.

This was not something she was ever supposed to find out about.

Something that I intended to keep private from her until the day I died. Maybe she would find old pictures or something after I was cold in the ground and think her mom really was something back in the day. Or maybe she'd be as disgusted with me as she is right now.

I feel dirty. Ashamed.

If there wasn't something wrong with me, we wouldn't be in this position. I'd never have left her father, and I'd never have married Billy, and Underwood never would have come into our lives and let his fucking kid overhear anything about this case.

My disgust turns to rage and I grip the steering wheel as tightly as I can. My joints pop as I do.

Olivia says nothing when we get home. She pours out of the SUV and slinks into the house, slamming the door behind her. And I'm sure that it's for me to see. She's furious. She's hurt.

My rage simmers into anger at myself. Disappointment with me. There's nothing like letting your child down.

You're supposed to be the person that protects them from the world. What happens when you're the one they need protection from?

I never thought I'd be in the position to find out.

The thought sends a fresh wave of nausea through

me. I know what comes next. What I have to do. And I don't want to.

But then I think that I deserve what I'm afraid of.

Michael should be angry with me. He has every right to be, just like our daughter.

I pick up the phone and call him.

"Hey, what's up?" He answers so casually. Unaware that I'm about to drop a bombshell on him.

"I think you should come over," I say.

My voice is hoarse, a shadow of its normal self.

"Are you alright?" There's concern in Michael's voice. Somehow that hurts worse than if he was yelling at me. In a moment, he won't be worried about me at all.

"I'm fine. It's Olivia. We need to talk," I tell him. "Please come over."

"Okay," Michael says. "Okay. I'm on my way."

We get off the phone, and I stare at mine on the counter for a moment. The screen goes black. The surrounding house is silent. I don't even hear Olivia's television in the other room, turned up way too loud so she can fight space aliens and zombies. I picture her in bed, turned to face the wall, curled in the fetal position.

I should go to her.

But I know she doesn't want me. She'll want her dad.

So, maybe the best thing I could do for her is what I just did. Maybe Michael will take her for the night.

Or maybe he'll take her forever.

The thought sends a chill down my arms and I shiver.

It's only a few minutes later when Michael knocks on the door. I'm so far lost in a trance about what a bad mother I am that I startle when he does. I'm brought back to the present and my stomach drops as I think about what I have to tell him when he walks through that door.

"Hi," I say as I swing it open for him.

"What's going on?" Michael asks, not bothering with smalltalk.

"Come in. Sit down," I say. "Do you want something to drink?" I ask, stalling.

"Kim, what's going on?" Michael doesn't sit down. "Is everything okay?"

Real fear is etched on his features. I feel like I'm being pulled down into a sandpit. Quicksand all around me, starting to nibble at my feet, snap at my ankles. I shift my weight back and forth, shaking it off.

"It's Olivia," I say. "She got into a fight today."

"Oh, my God," Michael says. "Was she defending herself?"

"No," I say.

"What?"

"A girl said something to her, and she punched the girl," I tell him robotically. This part is easy. This isn't the bad part. If this was it—that our child had reacted badly to being teased about something, maybe her appearance—it would be nothing. We'd deal with it head on, together. I don't know how to handle it with what really happened.

"What did the kid say to her?" Michael asks. He looks as confused as I was when the guidance counselor was breaking the news to me.

"I'm sorry, Michael," I say, a lump in my throat. "I failed her."

"Kim, what did the kid say?" Michael asks.

"The girl told her that her mom has sex parties," I say, spitting out the words and tasting the bile on every one. "She said, 'your mom is a swinger.'"

Michael is silent. It feels like forever. He doesn't react. His face goes blank. I can't read it.

"Which kid was this?" He asks.

"Hillary Underwood," I say. "As in a direct relation to Troy Underwood, I'm certain."

Michael runs a hand through his hair and then covers his mouth in disbelief.

"You think she could have overhead him talking about it?" he asks.

"I'm thinking that's what must have happened," I say. "The kid's gotta be his."

"Maybe not," Michael says. He looks at me, his eyes dark. "How many kids are talking about this, Kim?"

"I don't know," I admit.

"This is really bad. You know that, right?" He looks at me with a seriousness I haven't seen on his face since we got divorced.

"Of course, I know that," I say, folding my arms across my chest. "That's why I called you."

"Have you talked to Olivia about it?"

"Not yet. She won't even look at me," I tell him.

"Christ," he mutters.

"I was hoping you could get her to talk to me," I say softly.

He looks at me and anger flashes in his eyes.

"Kim, this is a big fucking deal," he says. "Olivia doesn't need to know about that stuff. She's still a kid."

"You think I don't get that?" I snap at him. "I've been

sick about it all day. I feel like the worst mother on earth. I feel like my kid will never be able to make eye contact with me again because I'm a dirty, disgusting whore!"

Michael's expression softens.

"You're not a whore, Kim," he says.

"I feel like one," I tell him. "I feel filthy."

He reaches for me, pulling me into an embrace.

I feel my body crumple against his. This softness is all I've craved all day. A safe place. A warm place. A person that doesn't hate me. That doesn't think I'm a horrible excuse for a human being, let alone a mother.

And then I start to sob.

"We'll navigate this," Michael tells me. "Like we've navigated everything. Let me talk to Olivia," he says and pushes me away slightly, looking into my eyes.

"Thank you," I say, hot tears streaming down my face. I swipe at them, not usually this vulnerable in front of anyone.

"We'll figure it out, Kim," he assures me.

And then he heads into the hallway and I hear the creak of Olivia's door as he opens it.

TWENTY-SIX

I CAN HEAR soft voices talking behind Olivia's door.

I hover in the hallway close by. A part of me hopes Michael will open the door and usher me in, Olivia having forgiven me and ready to make peace. I know that's unlikely, though. This will probably take time.

A lot of it.

I sigh and lean against the wall when I feel buzzing in my pocket. I fish out my phone and see a number I don't recognize. It's not Underwood, I think. Which is lucky for him.

I pick up the phone.

"Hello?"

"Mrs. Karlsen?" a soft voice on the other end asks.

"This is she," I say.

"Umm, this is Derek at the funeral home and I needed to talk to you because, umm—" he pauses, like he's searching for the right words. "Well, the check that you wrote us bounced."

"What?" I'm not sure that I'm hearing him right.

"When we deposited it, there wasn't enough money in the account you wrote it from to cover the balance of the funeral," he says. The words come out in a rush and he sighs, like he feels a sense of relief just getting them out there.

"I don't understand," I say.

The account I wrote the check from is the account that Billy has an automatic deposit set up on. The money comes directly from his business and goes into our account. I haven't looked at it in a week or so. But that's far from abnormal.

"I think there must be an error," I tell Derek when he doesn't say anything right away.

"That could very well be, ma'am," he says. But I can tell from his tone that he says this to everyone. And that most of the people he says it to are bullshitting him when they say there can't be a problem.

"We're good for it," I rush to tell him, suddenly feeling embarrassed for a whole new reason. "I mean, I'm good for it," I correct myself. "Umm, let me see what's going on with the account and I'll get back to you. Is that alright?" I ask.

"Of course," Derek says.

There's a note in his voice that makes me think he's not sure he's ever going to hear from me again.

How many people stiff a funeral home?

The thought horrifies me for a moment. I hang up the phone and my mind races.

Why the hell isn't there money in that account? Did something else come out that I wasn't counting on? Did the automatic deposits pause? Or did Billy have to do them manually? Was that just something I'd imagined?

The thoughts swim around each other and I'm ripped from the present moment. For a second, I forget that I'm waiting outside my teenager daughter's room, hoping that she won't be so ashamed of me that she refuses to look me in the eye for the rest of her life.

I stand there, dumbstruck.

It feels like everything is falling apart.

The only thing that could make this worse is if Underwood shows up to arrest me.

The thought of him sends fresh fury through me. I think about how upset Olivia was when I picked her up. How hurtful that must have been for her. I steam, imagining Underwood carelessly talking about the case in front of his kid. Her picking up on that and spreading it like wildfire among mean girls at the high school.

I want to set his lawn on fire and shit on his porch. All after I murder him in cold blood.

I take a deep breath, reminding myself that a dead body is what got us into this mess in the first place. I'm seething, though, at the thought of Underwood's smug smirk.

Finally, after what seems like a whole day, Michael emerges from Olivia's room.

"How'd it go?" I can't help myself from blurting the question out, even though Olivia can probably hear me. Michael ushers me into the living room, giving us—and Olivia—more privacy.

"She'll be okay," he says. "She's embarrassed, but she understands that not everyone is monogamous. I explained it to her the best I could. I was honest and tried not to go into too great of detail. She's upset. I'd give her the night to cool off."

I feel relief at his words. The thought that my daughter doesn't want to emancipate herself sets my ragged nerves back at a semblance of ease.

"What now?" I ask Michael.

He looks away, hedging whatever he's about to tell me. I search his face.

"She asked if she could stay with me tonight," Michael says.

My heart plummets to the soles of my shoes, shattering when it meets the tile below them.

"What?" I ask, barely audible.

"Just for tonight," he reassures me. "I think she just needs some space."

"Just tonight?" I ask, my voice sounding somewhat hysterical.

"Yes," Michael says, reaching for my arm. He squeezes it. "It's gonna be fine. Just give her a day to process this."

It feels like Michael shoved a knife into my hollow chest and twisted it. I never wanted to have a personal life that my kid would have to process.

"I think I'm going to throw up," I croak. Then I dash for the master bath.

I've got my head in the toilet, already on my second round of vomiting, when Michael catches up with me. He kneels by the toilet, pulling my hair away from my face.

"Don't be so hard on yourself," he says softly, his

voice barely above a whisper.

"Olivia is traumatized," I tell him. I vomit again.

"She's not traumatized, Kim," he says. "She's embarrassed. She'll get over it. She will. I know her. Hell, she's almost sixteen, and it's not like this is the first time she's ever been introduced to the idea that people have open marriages."

Shame races hot through my veins.

I was raised by a woman who thought drag queens were going to hell. A woman that thought that nonvirgin women wearing white on their wedding day were participating in false advertising. A woman who stood by her man even when the man hit her kid. It's no wonder the primary emotion around my sexuality is shame.

I throw up one more time for good measure and collapse against the tub when I feel like I don't have anything left in my body.

"It's gonna be okay, Kim," Michael says.

I nod, though I'm not sure how much I really believe him on this.

He places a hand on my thigh, leaning against the cabinets across from me. He pulls my feet into his lap, both of us sitting on the bathroom floor.

"Are you okay?" Michael asks.

"I feel better," I tell him. It's not a lie. I do feel better. Just the act of vomiting seemed to clear the shock of the day from my system. But then something else comes back to mind. "Oh," I say. "The funeral home called."

"What for?" he asks.

"The check I wrote bounced." The words come out

easily, simply. This isn't the worst thing that's happened today. Not by a mile.

"What?" Michael asks.

"I don't know," I tell him. "I need to figure out what's going on with Billy's accounts. I imagine he sent a payment to the account every month. And now that he's gone, no one's sending payments. And the office has been closed ever since he died," I say. "I'll figure it out tomorrow."

Michael nods, seeming to approve this plan of action.

"There's something more important I want to take care of first, though," I add.

Michael tilts his head.

"I'm going down to the police station and I'm talking to that bastard Troy Underwood about his asshole kid."

TWENTY-SEVEN

MICHAEL AND OLIVIA leave when I do, meaning that I'm coming home to an empty house. It's not something I look forward to, but the anger bubbling inside of me like a pot left to boil has me distracted. All I care about right now is talking to Underwood. More like ripping him a new asshole.

I speed across town, not caring if I get stopped. Finally, I pull up outside the police station, my tires screeching to a halt in front. An officer heading inside stops to look at me and I meet his gaze, unaided by my missing shades. I stare him down and eventually he turns and goes inside, probably not wanting to deal with the crazy woman who just pulled up at the station. I imagine they get that quite a bit. But I don't really give a shit.

I get out of the SUV and slam the door, making a beeline for the sliding glass doors.

Inside, I'm hit with a gust of air conditioning, but as soon as I pass the threshold, it's like there was never any A/C to begin with. The place is humid, and it has a smell. That's when I see a sign that says the air conditioner is out.

It doesn't matter to me. I don't plan to be here long.

I walk up to the window where a receptionist is piddling around with paperwork. I clear my throat and she takes a minute to bother to look up. When she does, she looks annoyed that I've materialized at her window. She slides it open.

"I need to see Detective Underwood," I say, not waiting for her to ask me what she can do for me.

"He's in the back taking his lunch. You'll have to wait," she says, and I swear that there's a degree of smug satisfaction in her tone.

"Oh?" I ask, my voice going dangerously high. "Is that back through there?" I point behind her.

Concern falls over her features, and she nods hesitantly.

I storm through the door that leads into the office space.

"Ma'am!" she shouts at me.

I grip my purse tighter and head to the back, toward a set of double doors that I imagine lead into a hallway that will take me where I need to go. Officers look up from their paperwork and phone calls, watching me as I pass. About as useless as they've proved to be during this whole investigation.

I crash through the double doors and see a sign that says Break Room. I throw the door open and step hastily inside. I see him immediately.

Sitting at the table with one of his cop buddies, he's eating a sandwich. Looks like the bastard is laughing about something with his friend, too. I storm up to him and slide into the seat across from him. I lean forward and slam my hand on the table to get his attention.

"Listen up," I say.

Underwood turns, shocked to see me. He lurches slightly in his seat.

"How did you get back here?" he demands.

"Did you talk about my husband's case in front of your kid?" I demand.

He looks bewildered.

"I imagine you'll be getting a call from your soon-to-be ex-wife, just like I got a call from the school this morning. My kid punched yours in the mouth. She made her bleed. And she deserved it. But not as much as you," I say.

"What the fuck are you talking about?" He's pissed now, leaning into the table just like me.

"Your kid told my kid that her mom's a swinger," I say. "There is exactly one way that little miss Hillary could know that," I say.

At the mention of his daughter's name, he sits back a little bit.

"Olivia wants to move. She's humiliated. She is fifteen goddamn years old, Detective," I say. "She still has to finish high school in this godforsaken town."

Realization seems to dawn on Underwood.

I can see the dots he's connecting. He talked about the case with someone while he was in front of his kid. She went to school and told all her little friends. And Olivia was automatically in their crosshairs.

"Kids will be kids," Underwood says.

"Because you said it in front of her," I snap.

"You need to get out of here, Mrs. Karlsen," he says. "This doesn't help your case."

"As far as I'm aware, you haven't arrested me yet," I say. "Rest assured, I'm lodging a complaint against you," I say. My lip trembles and I feel suddenly emotional. It's written all over his face how little he cares. It won't do anything. I feel my long-simmering rage starting to reach a boiling point. I stand up and lean closer. "Keep my kid out of this, asshole."

I turn on my heel and start to walk out. But then Underwood speaks.

"It's always the same kind of woman involved in these kinds of cases," he says, cool as a cucumber.

I stop but don't turn.

"I'm sure you know the kind I mean," he says. "Came from a broken home. Always needs a man's approval. I would imagine you're raising your daughter the same way," he says. "Maybe if you weren't, she wouldn't be so sensitive."

I feel a tear sneak down my face. I swipe at it and turn to face him.

"You know nothing about me," I say. "You're a jaded middle-aged burnout, unhappy with the trajectory of your life. Your wife is leaving you. And I can certainly see why."

Underwood's jaw tightens.

"And don't be shocked if, one day, your daughter does, too."

I turn and head back out of the police station.

MY HANDS ARE TREMBLING when I grab the steering wheel. I check twice to make sure the door is locked, part of me feeling like any moment, a bunch of cops are going to rush out to my car and arrest me. They'd probably be well within the law to do that.

But nothing happens.

It seems sort of indicative of the whole affair.

Nothing is happening.

Nothing good, anyway.

I sigh, slowly calming down. I back out of the spot and I head for the house, calling Michael on my way.

"Well?" he answers the phone. "I take it since you're calling me from your cell phone that you haven't been arrested." There's a note of playfulness in his voice. I fight back the urge to chuckle.

"Not arrested. *Yet*," I add.

"That yet is a very important qualifier," Michael says with a smile in his voice. "I take it you let him have it, though."

"As much as I could," I tell him. "Not that I think any of it really registered. I think cops like Underwood are untouchable. Or they think they are. In their mind, it's us versus them. There's no gray area."

"You're right about that," Michael says.

I'm not sure that he'd dare to disagree with me about anything right now. A smart man wouldn't. Michael's always been able to read me pretty well. It's not the time for a polite discussion on policing in America.

"How's Olivia?" I ask.

"She's fine," Michael says. "Getting settled in."

I don't say anything for a moment. I think about her leaving my house for his. Not that I begrudge them any of the time they spend together without me. It just cuts me to the quick to think that Olivia was so upset with me that she wanted to go to her dad's house.

It deflates me, leaching out my rage and replacing it with sorrow.

I clear my throat.

"Well, I'm headed to the bank to see what's going on with the accounts," I tell Michael.

"Have fun," he says.

"Yeah," I say, not in the mood for anymore teasing. I hang up the phone and head to the bank.

TWENTY-EIGHT

I PULL up out front of the bank at a quarter til five. They close at six, so it shouldn't be a problem. I hurry inside and take my place in line.

There are three lines, busier than it normally is on a weekday. At least before 5:00 in the evening. Not that I spend a lot of my time here. Finally, a spot clears at one of the teller windows and I step up.

"Hi," the girl says. She can't be more than nineteen. Olivia will be nineteen one of these days. It's hard to imagine her working at a bank, earning her own money, being out in the world without me to protect her.

Since I've done such a fine job of *that*.

I clear my throat.

"My name is Kim Karlsen and my husband—he passed away recently—we have an account here. I wrote a check for his funeral and the check bounced," I tell her, trying to be as concise as possible. The look on her face as she smacks a piece of gum lets me know that I wasn't nearly concise enough and if there was a way she could care less about my problem, she would have figured it out already.

"What's your account number?" Her voice is lazy as she asks the question. I feel myself getting irritated.

I rattle off the number to her. She types it into the computer and it takes her a moment to pull it up. After about five clicks of the mouse, she seems to have it on her screen.

"Yeah, looks like you're overdrawn," she says.

"I know that," I say, losing patience. "I want to know if there's a pending deposit from another account. External to the bank," I say.

She clicks around a little more with her mouse.

"Nothing that I can see," she says.

I sigh.

"So, there's nothing pending?" I ask.

"Nothing that I can see, like I said," she says. Now she's the one losing patience.

"Thanks," I say, grabbing my purse from the counter and turning on my heel.

There's only one place to look and I don't know if I have access to it.

Billy's computer.

I GET into the SUV and before I can even close the door, I'm sobbing.

The tears come hot and fast. Not the kind that you can choke back or hide. These are quick and furious, coming whether I want them to or not. I scream into the cabin of the car, and when I open my eyes, I see a couple on the sidewalk casting a dirty look at me in the driver's seat.

I grab the wheel and throw my head back against the seat rest.

What if there's no money left?

It brings to mind what Jackie told me initially after Billy was killed.

The note about the Blankenships and their money.

I wonder if they ever got it. The two of them haven't come knocking on my door.

I need to talk to them. As awkward as it would be, I need to ask them about that. But before I do that, I want to see if I can access his work files on the computer at home. I want to see if there's something in there that will tell me what the hell is going on with our money.

Billy has an account that receives all the dividends from his investments, plus the salary he gave himself at the financial advisory office. Usually, an amount is deposited into the account at the beginning of every month. But this month, it didn't arrive.

And I need to figure out if that's because he wasn't alive to put it in there, or because there's nothing left to transfer.

I head to the house and once I get there, I grab a half-eaten pint of Olivia's favorite ice cream. The name is a pun on some sitcom from the nineties. It's not my favorite, but I dig in, anyway. I want something that will numb me and ice cream works just about as well as anything.

I sit down in front of the television and find something that I can watch without having to concentrate. Another one of those housewives shows.

I finish the ice cream and cuddle up under the blanket on the couch. I snuggle down into the pillows and feel myself begin to drift off. And I don't wake until morning, when my phone is ringing off the hook.

I grab it, and the contact name shocks me into alertness.

It's Olivia.

TWENTY-NINE

"MOM?" Olivia's voice comes through the phone.

"Hey," I say, not taking my chances with a pet name or a diminutive. I feel lucky that she called me at all.

"I wanted to talk to you," she says.

My stomach ties itself in a knot. I don't know what she's about to say, but the possibility that she might want to live with her dad full time now crosses my mind in that instant. She's more than old enough to make that choice. And, even if I could, what judge would let me fight her given the circumstances.

I sigh.

"Okay."

"I talked to dad about everything. And I just want to tell you that I love you," she says.

I'm in shock at her words. I expected something different. I had braced for the worst. I don't exhale yet, though, knowing that there could be a but following that statement.

"He explained things to me and I don't want you to

think I don't love you because you're different," she goes on. "Because I *do* love you. No matter what. This all just...sucks," she finishes.

"Oh, baby," I say. "I love you, too. No matter what. And it's okay if you're angry with me and don't want to see me for a while," I tell her.

"No, it's not like that," she says. "I was just so hurt by what that bitch Hillary said. And I blamed you," she says.

Normally, I'd chastise her for her language. I don't have the energy, or maybe it's a gesture of goodwill on my part, trying to solidify this shaky olive branch she's sticking out for me.

I do notice with a smile that, if Michael's in the room with her, he hasn't bothered to correct her.

He did a better job of keeping his cool, but I know the whole thing pissed him off just as much as it pissed me off. Or possibly more.

"That's okay," I tell her. "So, what did your dad tell you?" I venture.

"He said that some people are monogamous and they only have one partner, but you're not monogamous. And you have more than one partner. And you always have," she says.

I sigh, a little relieved at the way he explained it.

I'm not sure what I expected, but Michael did a great job. I make a mental note to thank him.

"And I understand that it makes you different. And you and dad raised me that people shouldn't be made to feel bad because they're different. Remember how I had that gap in my teeth until I got braces?"

As if I could forget. The kids teased her mercilessly.

"Of course," I say.

"It's like that," she says.

I'm not entirely sure that Olivia's logic is perfectly sound, but I'm proud of her. Even though I still feel guilty. But I'll take it. Anything to put us back on a good footing. And I swear to myself right then that I'll spend the rest of my life making up for this. I hope it's enough.

"I'm ready to come back to your house tonight," she says.

I breathe a sigh of relief. It feels like a weight has been lifted off my chest. That she might never come back and call this place home had been weighing on me like an anvil on my sternum, making it hard to breathe. That she's not forsaking her home with me is good. Somehow, I don't feel like I deserve this kindness, though.

"I'd love that," I tell her, my voice coming out more quietly than I mean for it to.

"Dad said he'll bring me over as soon as he takes a shower," Olivia says.

"Y'all can take your time," I tell her, even though I'm eager to have her back.

We get off the phone and I mill around for a few minutes, not believing my good fortune that Olivia seems to have forgiven me for ruining her adolescence. I still feel like the biggest piece of shit imaginable.

After about thirty minutes, I hear Michael's truck in the driveway. The diesel engine shakes the walls of the house slightly, then he kills it. Everything goes silent until I hear the sounds of both doors closing. There's a knock at the door.

I get off the couch and spot Olivia's face pressed to

the carved glass in the center of the door. I laugh. It fills me with the sense that, no matter what else happens, we'll be okay.

"I'm coming!" I call to both of them.

Inside, Olivia makes a beeline for her room, ready to play video games on her own. Kids are more resilient than we think they are.

"How are you holding up?" Michael asks.

"Just glad that she's not refusing to ever stay with me again," I tell him. It comes out like an admission in a confessional booth. Quick, whispering.

"Oh, Kim, it's not that bad," Michael says.

"Somehow it feels that bad," I tell him.

"Stop beating yourself up," he says. "This is Underwood's fault."

On one level, I know he's right. On another, I think this wouldn't be an issue if I didn't live an alternative lifestyle. If I was normal. Maybe things would be easier for all of us if I was boring.

"Stop." Michael reaches for my arm and gives it a little squeeze. "I can see what's going through your mind and you need to quit it."

I smile at him, grateful for the grounding, even though I'm not sure I won't be back to beating myself up as soon as he's gone.

"Thank you," I say.

I appreciate the sentiment, no matter how hard it is to actually swallow.

Michael stays for a while and the three of us have dinner together. I order pizza and for a moment, as we all sit down at the table, it feels like old times. Michael and

Olivia joke with each other. Michael talks to me about all manner of things. Olivia chimes in. We talk about her college dreams. To all the world, we'd look like a normal family tonight.

Not one torn apart by divorce and murder.

But as I watch the evening unfold and the sun gets lower in the sky, I realize that we really aren't torn apart. Michael and I had an amicable divorce. The best kind for a kid. We're still good friends and we co-parent wonderfully. I've known women that have asked me how we do it, unable to stand the sight of their own ex-husbands.

And as I look at Michael across the table, lost in debate with Olivia about video games, I think the key might be to still be a little in love with your ex-husband.

Or at least the idea of what might have been could you have been someone else?

Someone that deserved him more.

Both of them.

I find myself not wanting to get up. Not wanting to clear our paper plates and throw out the cardboard pizza box. Maybe, just maybe, if I don't move, this moment won't end. I know this is the making of a memory. And we'll be transported somewhere else. Somewhere far away from the hellscape that we're currently navigating.

But Olivia gets up first, taking her plate to the trash can, and breaks the spell.

Michael smiles across the table at me. But there's no longer a protective bubble around us, keeping the reality outside at bay. There's a strain to his expression.

Olivia disappears down the hall, and Michael speaks.

"So, what happens next with the Billy stuff?" he asks.

"Well, I need to figure out how I'm going to pay for his funeral first," I tell him. Tension gathers at the base of my neck as I remember this tiny detail. We have no money. At least not until I figure out how to get into Billy's computer. I need to make sure there isn't money somewhere that I don't know about.

"Don't worry about it," Michael says with a wave of his hand. "I'll take care of it."

"Michael, I can't let you do that," I tell him sternly.

"I'm not doing it for you. I'm doing it for Olivia," he says simply. But we both know that's a lie. Michael would rescue me from just about anything. Even this.

"Michael," I say, treading carefully. "You know this hasn't changed anything, don't you?" I ask.

"Of course," he says, a little too quickly. I see a flash of pain in his eyes. The dashing of hope.

It makes me want to throw up all over again, that I'm the one who dashed it.

"I will always care about you," I say.

"And I'll always care about you, too, Kim," he says. His voice sounds almost defeated. Like it's his cross to bear.

"Well, I think we should call it a night," I tell him, standing from the table with my plate. "Can I take yours?"

"I'll get it," he says. But he stays at the table for a moment, seeming to contemplate something as I head to the kitchen and get started cleaning up.

AFTER MICHAEL LEAVES, I watch television for a little while. I can still hear Olivia in her bedroom, killing bad guys. Finally, I turn off the TV and head to her bedroom to say goodnight. Also to tell her that I don't expect her to go to school in the morning.

"Hey," I say, standing at her doorframe.

"Just a sec," she says, then sticks her tongue out in determination as she fights the big bad of whatever level she's on. "Okay," she says with a sigh of relief, having completed her mission for the night. "What's up?" she asks.

"I just wanted to talk to you," I say with a smile. "See how you're doing."

"I'm fine, mom. Really," she says.

"I was going to tell you that you don't have to go to school tomorrow if you don't want to," I tell her.

Olivia, normally tough, normally one to proclaim her toughness, is silent. A look of relief washes over her features. Like this was something she wanted but didn't dare to ask for. I feel it like a knife to the heart.

Olivia is scared to go back to school.

It's something she'd never say. But she doesn't need to. I can see it written all over her face.

"Okay," she says.

"Do you want to stay home?" I ask.

"Yeah," she says. "Maybe for a day or so," she adds, hoping to expand her absence.

I just nod, not wanting to commit to anything just yet. I'm unsure of what's best. For her to get some time away from school or for her to go back and confront her bully head on. I feel like I need to call a therapist.

There will be time for that when all of this is over.

Once they solve Billy's murder, it's straight to therapy for both of us.

"Mom," Olivia says, interrupting my train of thought. I look back up at her.

"Yeah?"

"Do you ever think about moving somewhere else?" she asks.

"Sometimes," I tell her. And if I was being totally honest, I'd add that I've thought about it a lot lately.

"What if we moved to the beach?" she asks.

I make a funny face and sort of smile in my confusion.

"You've never wanted to live at the beach," I say with a little laugh.

"I know, but I changed my mind," she says. "Remember all the times we went to the beach when I was a kid?" She asks, as though she's not still a kid.

"Of course," I say.

"We were all so happy there," she adds.

I feel a sinking sensation in my gut.

"What if we all just picked up tonight and left everything behind?" Olivia asks, hope in her eyes.

I realize that I'm about to quash someone's dreams for the second time tonight, and it doesn't make me feel anything other than rotten.

"Well," I say. "We can think about it. Why don't we get through this stuff with your step-dad first?" I ask, trying to soften the blow.

Olivia's face falls, but she nods, understanding it's impractical.

I step over and kiss her on the head. I squeeze her tight to me.

"Good night, sweetie," I say. "Things will be better in the morning."

And then I close her door behind me, and the tears start to fall.

THIRTY

I MAKE myself a cup of tea and I get antsy.

I think about Michael wanting to pay for Billy's funeral. How I really have no other choice but to let him. Unless there's money hiding somewhere I don't know about.

The thought eats at me until I head down the hallway to Billy's office.

I haven't bothered to get on the computer since he's been gone. Going into the study feels like disturbing a tomb. Like there's a part of me that's been preserving it for when he eventually comes home.

I step inside and switch on the lamp on his desk. It casts a glow around the room. It's almost spooky, the angle of the light casting high shadows up on the wall behind awards and trophies he's saved over the years. I hesitate, but sit down in the large chair behind the desk.

Sometimes I've used Billy's computer in the past for placing orders or shopping for things I don't need. I've also used it to check my email and keep up with social media at times. But mostly, I do those things on my phone.

I turn on the computer and it powers up, a musical note announcing that it's ready for me to login. The screen shows an avatar with his name under it, declaring that this is Billy's account and I need a password to access it.

I sit there, staring at the cursor. It blinks once, twice, a million more times as I stare at it. I try to think of what Billy used as a password for any of his accounts. I can't bring it to mind. It's a code of some kind. Something that he could use for any account and easily remember because it was a combination of letters and numbers changed slightly for whatever account he was accessing.

But I can't remember what the set of letters and numbers were that went into each password.

I try to search my memory for any combination that might be meaningful and I seize on the idea that it's our anniversary. That he changed it right after we got married. Shared it with me so I'd always know how to get into the accounts. It's our anniversary, plus our initials.

I type it in and add the word 'computer' to the end of it. I remember very clearly that our shared Spotify account had the same combo of letters and numbers with the word 'Spotify' following it.

I type it in confidently and hit enter.

The little avatar shakes from side to side, indicating the password is incorrect.

What?

I wonder if he changed it. Or maybe I typed it in wrong.

I type it again, more carefully this time, looking at each key as I hit it.

Still wrong.

Billy has always used the same kind of formula for his passwords. I wonder if, when things got rocky between us, he changed some of them from our anniversary to something else.

He had told me the password was always what or who was most important to him in his life. I think about the images of Nicole that he had hidden in his desk. I type out the same combination but add her name at the end.

The little icon shivers again, telling me I got it wrong.

A warning pops up. Two more tries and then I'm locked out.

On a whim, I type out the password and add Lindsay's name at the end.

Almost as I expected, the icon dances around. Wrong again.

I think hard about it for a moment. And then it comes to me, plain as day. The only person he really cared about was Olivia.

I try her name with the combination, and the screen unlocks.

I exhale, glad that it worked, unsure of what the hell I would have done if it hadn't.

I sit there for a moment, just staring at the home screen and being grateful that I got this far. I wonder if he changed his other passwords to her name, too.

If he did, this should be pretty easy.

I open his browser and go to his favorites. I see the name of our bank. I click on it and type in the login information. It works, and the screen is filled with the loading icon. It takes a few seconds, and then the accounts pop up. The one we share is at the top. He has others. I know he has a savings account of his own and another checking account for business stuff. But I'm shocked to see that there are a few others.

Ones I didn't know about.

And all of them are in the *negative*.

The savings account is drained, too. So is the business checking account.

I look again at his favorites tab. I go to one that leads to his investments. The account that our monthly payment comes from.

I log in with the same password.

And I almost throw up when I see the number on the screen.

The reason there was no transfer this month is because the amount transferred each month was more than $6,000. And the account only has $523.21 left in it.

All of our money is gone.

Where in the hell did it go?

My heart hammers in my chest. The thought that Billy was keeping this from me is maddening. What the hell was he doing?

Just leave? Was he going to disappear?

He got lucky and got murdered.

He doesn't have to deal with the fallout.

It briefly makes me wonder if he killed himself. I

think about the bruising on his face. How it looked like he'd been in a fight. I doubt he really did it himself.

Still, the reality remains: we have no money.

And I don't know what we're going to do.

THIRTY-ONE

I SIT in the chair in Billy's office for a moment, unsure of what to do.

I grab my phone and dial Amanda's number, suddenly struck with an idea. It rings four times and then goes to voicemail. She's not taking my call.

I dial it again, and again, and on the fourth try, Amanda answers after the first ring.

"Hello?" she says into the receiver. Her voice is unsure. Not the usual Amanda that's making deals in boardrooms, controlling a crowd of good ol' boys. No, this Amanda seems scared that I even have her phone number. What do they think of me?

Do they think I did it?

"Amanda," I say. Her name comes out in a rush. So do the words that follow. "I need to talk to you about something. It has to do with Billy. Billy and the financial investment office, I mean."

"Okay," she says cautiously.

"Can I come over?" I ask, not even bothering with any form of politeness.

"Umm—" I hear a voice in the background, surely Dan asking her who's on the phone at this godawful hour.

She must cover the receiver. I hear muffled voices. They go back and forth for a minute. Finally, she returns.

"Sure," she says.

The word has a degree of curiosity in it.

"Be there soon," I say, and then I hang up the phone.

I check and make sure that Olivia's asleep and I drive over to Dan and Amanda's house. I get out of the car and straighten my shirt before I knock on the door, suddenly aware that I haven't had a shower in a couple of days. That's not like me.

The stress of everything is getting to me.

I knock on the door, three raps.

Amanda answers it immediately, like she was standing on the other side, waiting for me to get out of the car and come up their walk. Unnerved, I jerk my hand back, still in mid-air.

"Come in," she says quickly.

I dart into the house, for some reason not wanting to give Underwood any further ammunition. I could see him being inquisitive as to why I'd been at the Blankenships' house after ten on a weeknight.

"What's going on?" Amanda asks as I step into the living room.

"I need to ask you about something," I tell her. "About the money that Billy owed you."

Amanda furrows her brows.

"What money?" she asks.

"There was a note on his desk. $155,000 with your last name next to it."

Amanda looks confused. Dan appears from around the corner.

"What's this about?" Dan asks. He's on the defensive already, probably wondering what the hell I'm doing here at this hour.

I don't really blame him.

I'd be asking the same question were the roles reversed.

"Did Billy owe the two of you some money?" I ask.

"No," Dan says. "Why?"

"There was a note indicating an amount next to your last name," I tell him.

"Oh," Dan says. "Well, we invested with him."

"$155,000?" I ask.

"Yeah," Dan says. "We invested that with him."

"So, he didn't owe you anything?" I ask.

"No," he says.

I feel cold sweat break out on my forehead. I debate telling them the truth. I should. I should tell them everything. They deserve to know.

"I think there's a problem," I say hesitantly. Part of me doesn't even want to go there.

It's not in my best interest. But it's the truth.

"What's wrong?" Amanda asks.

"I don't think the money is there," I say.

Dan's face goes pale.

"What do you mean?" Amanda asks.

"All of our money is gone," I say, spitting it out.

Dan chokes back a laugh.

"You can't be serious," he says.

"Dead," I say.

"How do you know?" he asks.

"I got into Billy's computer a little while ago. I never use it. The only account I ever look at is the one we share. The one that we pay our bills out of. That I go grocery shopping with. The one I wrote the check for his funeral out of."

Dan stares at me, waiting for further explanation.

"The check bounced. The funeral home called me and told me," I say. "I started doing some digging, and it doesn't look good."

"Oh, my God," Dan says, covering his face with his hands.

"The police are checking his work computer now, so I'm sure they're going to find this. If he owed you money, you need to be honest with them about it," I say.

"He didn't owe us anything!" Amanda says.

"So, you didn't kill him?" I ask, point blank.

"Kill him?!" Dan asks, incredulous. "We had nothing to do with that. We thought you killed him."

"I didn't kill him," I say plainly. "But, Amanda," I say. "Why were you buying burner phones at the super center?"

"We use them on vacation," she says simply and shrugs. "The detective asked about that. We usually get international SIM cards and then just throw them into the prepaid phones."

"It's cheaper than calling from our regular lines," Dan explains.

My mind swims. If that's true, then they really

haven't done anything suspicious. Who hurt Billy if it wasn't Dan and Amanda over the money?

My mind drifts to Nicole.

Could Jason have wanted Billy out of the picture after he found out that his wife was having an affair with him?

I feel a swirl of emotions inside me. I don't know what to think.

"So, you didn't even get in a fight with him?" I ask Dan.

"No," Dan says. "I was with Nicole that night. Amanda was with Jason. And you and Jackie and Nathan were outside."

I reel, unsure of what to think.

"Jesus," I mutter.

"Do you want a cup of coffee or tea or anything?" Amanda asks, no longer looking like she's afraid of me. Now she looks like she feels bad for me.

"No," I say. "I've already taken up too much of your time."

I don't know what I'm going to do when the cops come to my door telling me that Billy owed real investors a lot of money.

I FEEL sick as I drive home. The implications of what's coming wash over me.

When the cops figure this out, we're going to lose the house eventually. We will have to start over, Olivia and I, on our own.

I hate myself.

This is all my fault. There are a million ways I could have prevented this. I could have been more in tune with what was going on at Billy's office. I could have monitored the accounts. Known what was in them. I could have been different. More insistent on knowing the details of things. A better person. A better mom. Not anything like who I really am.

I sit in the driveway, crying for several minutes, until my face is red and puffy and my eyes are bloodshot.

As I walk in, I take in every detail of the house. I recall good memories. Times when things were better between Billy and I. Times when Olivia was here. Christmas, New Year's. Parties we threw. Happy times. All of that gone tonight.

I don't know what to think.

I don't know quite what to do.

And then I slip into bed, wondering who killed my husband, but thinking I might have an idea why.

THIRTY-TWO

THE NEXT MORNING, I wake up with one thing burning in my mind. The thought of Nicole having an affair with Billy. There's no way that Jason didn't kill him. Or at least be the one that assaulted him before he died.

I contemplate going over there tonight, confronting them about it.

But I know my best course of action is to leave it to the professionals, no matter how much I don't trust them. Underwood in particular.

I need to keep cooperating with him, though, if I ever want to get out from under this.

I pick up the phone and call him.

"Detective Troy Underwood," he says into the phone.

"It's Kim," I say, knowing that by now, we're on a first name basis. Or at least he is with me. I'm not sure I want to chance calling him Troy.

"Mrs. Karlsen," Underwood says, mock joviality in

his voice. "Just who I wanted to hear from. How are you this morning?"

"I'm fine," I tell him, eager to cut to the chase. "I just wanted to see where things stood with Nicole Phelps and my husband."

"You want to know if she killed him? Or her husband killed him because you think the two of them were having an affair?" he asks.

There's a note in his voice that annoys me. I know he's not taking me seriously. I can tell he's looking at this as an effort on my part to divert attention from myself. I sigh into the phone, trying to collect myself. Trying not to have an outburst.

"Basically, yes," I say.

"Mrs. Karlsen," Underwood says. His voice drips with patronization. "You'll be the first to know when there's a break in this case."

"So you don't think they had anything to do with it?" I ask, losing some of my cool.

"No, I don't," Underwood says.

"Why not?" I ask. "They have the motive. They had the opportunity."

"And nowhere in the Phelps' house did I find a roofie. Or any drug like it," Underwood cuts in. So they didn't have the means. Or at least we can't prove they had the means."

"So?" I feel on the verge of hysteria.

"We need motive, means, and opportunity for a case, Mrs. Karslen," he says, explaining this to me like one of Nicole's kindergarteners.

"I know that," I snap. "I'm just saying you need to look at it again."

"I talked to Mr. and Mrs. Phelps," he says. "Both of them vehemently denied any involvement on her part with your husband. They offered their cell phones and not once was there a call from Billy to Mrs. Phelps," Underwood says.

It makes no sense.

"They could have used burner phones," I say, like Underwood is a moron.

"They could have," he admits. "But we have little reason to think they did at this point."

"What about those pictures with her in them?!" I almost shout.

"It can't be proved that those are Nicole Phelps. She said the anklet is hers but she has no memory of taking the pictures and hasn't worn the anklet in years. When we searched the house, it wasn't there."

"Search it again!" I scream into the receiver.

I know I sound crazy. I feel like I'm losing it.

I sense someone standing in the doorway and look over. I spot Olivia, watching me with wide, terrified eyes. I gesture for her to wait. She does so, but I can tell she's frightened. I've scared her.

"Mrs. Karlsen," Underwood says. "It came to our attention via the forensics department that your husband was in a bind financially. It's also come to my attention that you were the sole beneficiary on his life insurance policy. Billy was committing widespread fraud with his investors. I think you strongly need to consider the possibility that it's time for you to come clean with us."

I sit there, aghast.

Did he just say that to me?

"You mean confess to a crime I didn't commit?" I ask sharply.

"I didn't say that," Underwood says, cagey as fuck.

"You heavily implied it," I say.

And then I hang up on him.

I ball my fists at my side and grab a pillow, screaming into it before I remember Olivia is standing there. I put it down and turn to face her.

"Honey, I'm sorry," I say. "Things are just getting complicated with what happened to Billy."

She looks like she wants to know what's going on, but is afraid for me to tell her. Like it's just one more thing that will turn her reality upside down again.

"Come here," I say, my tone softening. I reach out my arms for her.

She comes over and gives me a hug. I tug on her hand and she sits down on the bed beside me.

"Is everything okay?" Olivia asks.

"It's fine, honey," I tell her. It's a lie.

I have no idea how long it'll be before we have to sell the house. Eventually, Olivia will be privy to all the information. I can't shield her from it forever, but I wish I could. I'll do my best.

"You seem upset," she says.

"I am," I admit. "I just want them to get this all figured out," I offer her a smile. It's half-hearted, though. And she picks up on that.

"Do you think they're going to solve it?" she asks.

"I don't know, honey," I tell her. It's the truth. I'm not sure if we'll ever know what happened.

She nods, seeming to accept this. Probably not understanding fully what that will mean for the rest of her life. Wondering forever who hurt her step-dad, someone she truly cared about. But for now, she seems okay with the idea.

I wonder how long that will last, though.

I scoop her into a hug and squeeze her tight, finding myself wishing she was little again. Too little to really understand what was going on around her. What had happened, and what was coming.

I let go of her, and she stands up.

"I love you, Mom," she says, and heads back out into the main part of the house.

"I love you, too," I say after her.

I hear her pad into the living room and down the other hallway, and then I hear her door shut. I imagine she'll spend the day lost in video games. Which is fine. I'd rather she do that than stew about what's being said at school right now. I don't want her to go back. I want Underwood's kid taken out. Punished. Olivia shouldn't be the one that's suffering.

I feel fresh rage bubbling in my veins.

Maybe I need a day to give my mind a break.

It seems like there's just been one thing after another ever since this whole thing started. First it was Billy, then the affair, then Olivia, and now the money.

I grab my phone and shoot off a text message to Jackie, the only other person I know to not be at work right now.

Wanna come over and drink by the pool?

She writes back almost instantly.

Kimmie, you're speaking my language. See you in 10.

I get up and put on my swimsuit, then head to the kitchen to wait for Jackie.

THIRTY-THREE

JACKIE SHOWS UP, and I recognize the shades on her face instantly.

"Hey, I've been looking for those," I say with a laugh.

She looks at me bewildered for a moment, then realizes I'm talking about the sunglasses.

"Oh, shit," she says. "I must have mistaken them for mine. I have a pair just like them."

She hands them over to me.

"What's on the agenda today?" she asks.

She wears a cover up over a gold bikini that ties at the waist, neck and back. Her raven hair is pulled up and held back by a blue bandana. She looks the picture of summer in Texas. She even smells like coconut, and I assume she lathered up with sunscreen before she came over. Jackie, even though she's darker than I am, is always conscious about taking care of her skin. More conscious than me by a long shot.

"You smell fantastic," I say, leaning in to smell the

coconut on her shoulder. "I thought we'd just chill today. I think I need it."

"I could have told you that," Jackie says with a laugh. "I'm down."

"I'm going to make us a couple of margaritas and I'll meet you outside."

"I'm going to use the bathroom," Jackie asks.

I nod, and she disappears down the hallway with her bag. I hear the door shut and I get to work on the drinks.

Jackie reappears, sans bag or cover up, only clad in her bikini and flip-flops. I grab the drinks and we head out to the patio. We snag two chairs next to the pool, and I place the margaritas between us.

Jackie sits down and takes a sip of hers.

"Oooh, strong," she says. "Just the way I like it."

"I know," I say with a smirk. "Me, too."

She smiles at me.

There's something warm about Jackie. Her smile. Her body language. Everything about her is inviting. My mind drifts to all the times we'd been left almost alone together at one of our parties. How there was a flittering of nerves that I never got with any of the guys. Butterflies, I guess you could say. And Jackie seemed to know it.

"So, what's on your mind?" Jackie asks.

I snap back to the moment and clear my throat, suddenly feeling like she might have the power to read minds.

"Oh, not really anything," I lie.

"You're in the middle of a murder investigation," Jackie says. "You've got to have something on your mind."

I laugh. She's right.

"I found out we have no money," I tell her. "The firm has no money. They think Billy was making bad investments and lying to people. The detective told me. I have no idea what's going to happen."

Jackie looks taken aback.

"What?" she asks.

"I don't know how it happened, but Billy had no money. There was practically nothing in the accounts. It's only a matter of time before people come asking for it and the house gets taken out from under us."

"Jesus Christ, Kim," she says. "That's terrible."

"I've weathered worse," I tell her, thinking about all the times my mom had to move us when I was a kid and she just wasn't paying rent or utilities wherever we lived. Olivia and I would make do. I'd work however I had to for a roof to put over her head.

It pained me to think of losing the house, but my eyes drifted to the pool.

I hadn't been able to get in the water since we found Billy's dead body floating in it.

Maybe it would be good to start over.

"What's the detective saying these days?" Jackie asks.

"Nothing important," I say, irritated at the very mention of Underwood. "I think he's got his mind made up about the whole thing. You could probably show him a video of the President killing Billy and he'd still think I had something to do with it."

"But he's got no evidence of that, right?" Jackie asks.

"Of course not," I say, almost defensively.

I'm almost offended that Jackie has to ask. She was

there with me. She saw me find Billy's body. She was party to it.

"He's just hung up on it," I say. "You know, like on one of those crime shows where the cop gets one thing in his head and can't fathom being wrong."

"Oh, yeah," Jackie says. "I know what you mean."

I settle back in my chair and sip my margarita. We talk about life, men, and all the bullshit surrounding the case about Billy. I tell her about what happened to Olivia at school. She's enraged and wants to give Underwood a piece of her mind.

At around noon, Jackie gets up and decides she wants to take a dip in the pool. She goes to the diving board and I stay on the sidelines, watching from my lounge chair.

The pool was chemically cleaned right after we found Billy. But still, the water feels dirty to me. I don't want it on my skin, but I don't share that with Jackie. I don't want to dampen the mood. She's excited to swim and I'll let her remain that way.

She leaps from the board and does a cannonball. It splashes me all the way up at the shallow end where the chairs are. I laugh, guarding my margarita from more fallout. She pops out of the water; the liquid glistens like glitter on her brown skin.

I want to reach out and touch it. But that would require getting into the water.

Her hair is slicked back on her head, her bandana lost somewhere in the pool when she jumped in. She smiles at me, her teeth Instagram white.

She could be a model, I think.

I figure it's one reason that Nathan agreed to swing.

Jackie is gorgeous. Nathan is average. I wonder if he was afraid there was no way he could keep her unless he gave in to her whims. It's a nasty thought, but it's mine nonetheless.

I could see how it could have gone the other way, too. Maybe a man less secure would have thrown a fit about Jackie wanting to live that lifestyle. Maybe Nathan did. Just like Billy toward the end, wanting me to fit my square peg into a round hole that would make him more comfortable.

I remind myself that I don't need to worry about any of that today. Today is about taking the time to breathe. To relax in the middle of all of this. I need to or I'm going to have an aneurysm. I take a deep breath in through my nose, exhaling through my mouth like I'm in some kind of meditation class.

"Come in!" Jackie says.

She dunks her body up to her chin.

"I don't think I want to," I tell her.

"It feels great," she says. She dips down a little further and gets some water in her mouth. She makes a raspberry and blows it at me, sprinkling me with a fine mist.

"Jackie!" I shout, but I'm laughing.

There's a part of me, though, that can't help but feel that part of that little shower contained fragments of Billy. Dead skin cells, though sanitized, might still remain in the pool. I needed to have it drained, the lining replaced, and refilled, not just chemically cleaned.

Something I could do if I only had the money. Something that's laughable now.

I look at Jackie in the shallow end. She beckons me with her finger.

I give in and get up. I head to the steps.

"No," she says. "Jump off the diving board."

"What is this? Sixth grade?" I tease. "What does it matter how I get in?"

"If you jump off the diving board, you'll be all wet just like me," she says.

The words hang between us, the double entendre not lost on me. I swallow, suddenly feeling nervous. My mouth is dry. I look away, but I do as she says, heading for the diving board. I step up onto it and look down at the pool below. I think about Billy floating in the deep end, unnoticed for how long?

The thought chills me despite the relentless heat in the air around me.

I look at Jackie once more. She gives me an encouraging nod.

I think about all that's been lost. I think about the uncertain future ahead. How all of this has and will affect Olivia for a long time to come. I think about her idea that we move to the beach.

And then I take a deep breath and jump, wrapping my arms around my shins and making the biggest splash I can.

Even though it's hot, the water is cold on my skin. Instantly refreshing, a shock to my system. I bob up in the deep end, gasping for air and laughing. Jackie was right. It was better this way.

I swim toward her and she reaches out for me wordlessly. She takes my hand in hers and interlaces our fingers. And then she pulls me against her, our chests colliding. I can feel her erect nipples as a breeze sweeps across the pool.

She kisses me, crushing her mouth to mine.

We've never done this. Not alone. Not behind anyone's back. But if I'm being honest with myself, I've longed for it. I get the impression that she has, too. I think about all the times she made eye contact with me from across a party, the implied message being that she wished we were alone. I had felt it, too, even if I hadn't understood it.

I kiss her back, and her hands are at my back, untying my bikini. She slips hers off, bottoms, too. And I do the same.

Her hands slide up my thighs, finding the spot instantly. I gasp. Jackie leans forward, working her hand against me. It's only a moment before I climax, all of the tension built up between us over the years serving as foreplay. I try to catch my breath. She's smiling at me, pressing her forehead against mine. She kisses me there.

"You're so beautiful, Kim," she whispers.

I'm still in shock. Utter shock that we did this. Behind Nathan's back. And even though Billy is dead, it feels like we did it behind his back, too. Or right on top of him, which seems even worse.

I have to look away from her face. I'm ashamed.

Not just that we've broken the rules, but by something else. Some other part of myself that I've denied for so long.

I finally meet her gaze again and laugh nervously.

"Are you okay?" she asks. Her tone turns frantic, almost. She thinks she's done something wrong.

"I'm fine!" I assure her. "I just—"

"I've wanted to do that for a long time," Jackie admits.

I struggle to speak. I've wanted it, too.

"Same," I say.

She draws near to me and kisses me. Gently this time. My hands find themselves tangling in her hair. I want to pull her closer, closer, until we're melded together. One body, so she can never leave me. So that whatever comes next, at least we're together.

But she pulls away, naturally. She looks into my eyes.

"Are you sure you're okay?" she asks.

"I am," I reassure her, though I don't know if it's the truth. "Do you want another margarita?" I ask her, trying to break the tension and retrieve some sense of normalcy. I have no idea what to do with what I'm feeling right now.

She nods and I head for the stairs. She follows me out onto the sidewalk around the pool and grabs her towel from her lounge chair. I head inside and get started making us two fresh margaritas, complete with salt on the rim and a lime wedge.

Jackie comes in at some point, wrapped in her towel, and heads to my bathroom.

I say nothing to her, unsure what sure what to say. I don't want to ruin the magic of what just happened. But I don't know how to take it any further. It feels like unfamiliar territory. And I want to explore it.

A voice in the back of my mind tells me it's not the appropriate time. Or place. My kid is in her bedroom. I don't need to be embarking on an affair before my husband is cold in the ground. Jesus Christ.

I head back out onto the patio and soon, Jackie comes back out, too, bag on her shoulder. Now she's wearing her cover up and her hair is pulled once again into a bun. I think again about how gorgeous she is.

She sits down next to me and gratefully takes her second margarita. She kicks off her sandals and slips her feet up onto the lounge chair. She places her bag on the ground and it falls over. Something falls out, and I see it glint in the sun. My eye is naturally drawn to it.

An anklet.

And it has a horseshoe charm.

THIRTY-FOUR

I STARE at the charm in disbelief for a second.

"Jackie," I say her name. It comes out, tasting like something foreign to my tongue. I feel like I've never known her. Like she's a stranger sitting next to me that just got me off in a swimming pool. The harsh realization of what's happening hits me like a rogue wave.

"Hmm?" she asks. She's blissfully unaware.

"Where did you get that?" I ask her, pointing at the anklet on the ground.

"Oh, I've had that for a while," she says, but it rings false.

"Jackie, did you have an affair with Billy?" I ask.

The words come out like a ton of bricks. They plop down between us, a heavy thud in the conversation. She sits up.

"What?" she asks.

"I've seen that anklet," I tell her. "I thought it was Nicole's. But it was in your bag. I saw it in the pictures I found in his desk," I say, mentally putting the pieces together.

I think about the shades she just gave back to me. How things would sometimes go missing and reappear. Once, how Jackie told me she had a shoplifting problem when she was younger. I wonder if she stole the anklet from Nicole.

It had never been Nicole.

It had always been Jackie.

Jackie had the affair with Billy.

Nathan killed him.

I stand up, shocked by my own thoughts. Jackie stands up and walks toward me. I hold out a hand, suddenly feeling sick that I let her into my house. And with Olivia here. What could happen?

Jackie holds up both her hands.

"Calm down, Kim," she says. "It's not what you think."

"Jackie, those photos I showed you were of you."

She swallows, caught in a lie.

"I can explain," she says. "I thought it was better that way."

"To lie and act like you had no idea about those pictures?" I ask, incredulous.

My life is crumbling around me.

"Billy and I never had an affair," she says.

"It was a one-time thing?" I ask, still indignant that they would keep it a secret. That wasn't fair. That wasn't the rule we played by.

"Nothing like that happened," Jackie swears. "Just listen to me."

"Why should I?" I ask, sounding hysterical.

"Because your husband wasn't the person you thought he was," she says plainly. "He was a monster, Kim."

I stand there, shocked by her words. Billy could be harsh, but he wasn't a bad person. He'd made some mistakes with the money, sure. And he wasn't always the greatest to me. But he'd been a good step-dad. A good coach for Olivia's school. He was always ready to volunteer to help people when they needed it. A *monster*? I hardly think so.

I feel like Jackie is trying to throw me off the scent.

"Did Nathan kill him?" I ask her, point blank.

She looks like I've just thrown cold water on her. The shock she's feeling is palpable.

"Are you kidding?" she asks.

"No, I'm serious, Jackie. What happened?"

"Billy forced me to take those pictures," she says. "It wasn't long after he hired me. He found out some stuff about me. I guess he had a private eye look into my background when I came to work for him. Anyway, he held this secret over my head. Told me if I didn't do what he wanted, he would tell Nathan everything. He made me go to events with him and everything. And I couldn't have that," she says. Her tone is coated with deadly seriousness.

"What was the secret?" I ask, realizing that it must have been Jackie in the Facebook photo Amanda had shared, just out of the viewfinder, off to the side.

"I don't want to talk about it, Kim," she says. Her tone

pleads with me to drop it, but I feel like I have a right to know.

"Tell me what the secret was. What was so bad that you took these pictures for him?" I ask. I can't imagine Billy doing that. It wasn't like him. He didn't even like the idea of me sleeping with other men, even if he got to sleep with other women at the same time. He was too strait-laced.

"Kim, it really doesn't matter," she says, a last ditch effort.

"Tell me," I say.

"I have a child," she admits.

Shock washes over me anew.

"A child?" I ask.

"Yes," she says. "My ex has full custody. I don't get to see her. I send her stuff sometimes. He sends me pictures. I'll never be a part of her life. That was a dark time when I had her. I was strung out on stuff. I was automatically an unfit mother."

"Jesus, Jackie," I say, digesting this.

"Nathan doesn't know. He can't know," she says. "It would never be the same between us, and I love him."

"Billy found this out and used it against you?" I ask.

I'm shocked. Utterly confounded.

Realization starts to dawn on me.

"Yes," Jackie says. "He made me strip down and take those pictures right there in the office. He got off on the power of it."

I start to feel sick. Weightless. The room starts to spin.

"Jackie," I say. "Did you do something to Billy?"

She looks at me, battered emotionally from the confession she's just made. It's the only logical conclusion. I would have been ready to kill someone who had done the same to me. Especially if it threatened my own marriage.

Forlorn, she speaks.

"No, Kim. I didn't kill him. And neither did Nathan. They got into it in the garage when we first got to your house. Billy thought we were alone and started in on me. He grabbed my wrist. Nathan walked in on us. He threatened Billy. Punched him in the face. Billy made himself a whiskey, took the whole bottle with him, and went into his study. That was the last time we saw him."

I mull this over. They didn't kill him. I believe her.

But if they didn't, who did?

THIRTY-FIVE

JACKIE LEAVES, and I lean against the door as she starts up her convertible and heads down the street. I stand there until I can't hear it anymore. Until it disappears like it was never here to begin with.

I think about calling her to come back. To tell her that we need to share this with Underwood. But what good would it do? It would make Jackie and Nathan look suspicious. But what if Billy had done this to other people?

There were no other people at the house that night, though.

I'm reeling from this information.

Was my husband a monster?

Could I really not have known that?

I think about the picture that I saw on Amanda's Facebook. How I wondered who the woman just off to the side was. How could it have been Jackie, and I didn't know?

I feel like I'm going to be sick.

I head to the kitchen and grab my phone, thinking

that it's time to follow up with Billy's sister. I want someone to tell me that they can't reconcile this information with who this man was. I want her to tell me he'd never have done such a thing, but they haven't been in touch in years.

How much could she possibly know?

I don't care. I need to know.

I dial Lindsay and my heart flutters in my chest as it rings. I pace the kitchen tile and she answers.

"This is Lindsay," she says into the receiver.

"Hi, Lindsay, this is Kim. Your brother's wife," I say, though I'm not sure I needed to reintroduce myself.

"Oh, Kim!" She sounds happy to hear from me. "I'm glad you called. I was actually planning on calling you."

"Really?" I ask.

"Really," she says.

I hesitate for a moment. She fills the silence.

"I just wanted to check on you, see how you're doing," she says.

"It's a nightmare, if I'm honest," I say with a dark chuckle. For some reason, I feel like I can be totally honest with her. She doesn't make any sound, but I hear her exhale.

"I'm so sorry," she says. "I should have known it would be something like this."

"What do you mean?" I ask her.

"That he would meet a sticky end," she says. "The police are involved, aren't they?"

There's something frosty about her voice.

"Yes," I say, somewhat hesitantly. Suddenly, I don't feel as comfortable sharing so much with her. I remind myself that she isn't a girlfriend I've known since junior high.

This is a woman whose existence I wasn't aware of until just recently.

"Can I ask you something, Lindsay?"

"Sure," she says, her tone suddenly warmer.

"Why have you been following me?"

"Well, I was afraid to approach you at first. I didn't know how you'd react. I wanted to know the woman my brother had married, and—"

"There's more to it than that, isn't there?" I ask.

She seems to hesitate.

"Can you meet me somewhere tonight?" Lindsay asks.

"Sure," I say. "Anywhere."

I realized instantly after I say it that it might not have been the right thing to say. I don't want to meet her in some back alley. I don't know this woman.

"What about the parking lot of the super center?" I suggest.

"That's perfect. See you soon," she says and hangs up.

I PULL up into a spot under a huge streetlamp. I told Olivia I'd only be gone for a little while, assuring myself that nothing bad is going to happen and I'll be back in the safety of my home soon.

Or at least what's going to be my home for a few more weeks.

I have no idea what's going to happen with all of that.

Suddenly, I see Lindsay's black sedan pull into the spot next to mine. She gets out and comes and gets into the passenger side of my SUV.

"Hey," I say.

"Hi, Kim," she says.

"So," I say. I feel like a teenager about to make out for the first time. The tension in the air is thick enough to spread across bread.

"Well, the real reason I was trying to work up the courage to talk to you is because I wanted to know something," she says. "When I found out you had a daughter, I thought it was important that I speak to you about some things."

My chest tightens.

I hate the fact that she's bringing Olivia into this. It makes me sick. How have I messed up so badly?

"Billy and I were very close when we were little," she says. "He was my older brother and I looked up to him in so many ways," she smiles at the memory. "He was a good person in his heart."

I remain silent, afraid to speak.

"But when he turned fourteen, that's when things changed," she says.

She seems to gather herself, as though what she's going to tell me next is hard for her.

"When I was about eight years old, Billy touched me for the first time," she says. "It continued until we were well into our teens. I didn't realize what it was when I was a kid. I loved him so much," she says. A tear streaks her cheek. The light from the pole next to us illuminates it, making it glitter in the night.

"Lindsay," I say. I'm unsure how to continue.

But she goes on, preventing me from having to think too much about it.

"I just—I just wanted to make sure he hadn't done that to your daughter," she says. She makes eye contact with me for the first time since getting into the car.

"No, he didn't," I tell her.

But even as the words come out of my mouth, doubt creeps into my mind. How could I not have suspected him of being a monster?

With what he did to Jackie, this makes sense.

Jesus. I need to talk to Olivia.

"Are you sure?" she asks.

I hesitate.

Because I'm *not* sure.

I GO HOME and I see Michael's truck in the driveway.

The door leading into the house is unlocked. Michael let himself in.

He doesn't usually do that, but it's not quite that surprising. Sometimes he would when Billy was out of town for work. There's something about it that's inappropriate and comforting at the same time. Michael has really stepped up for me the last week or so.

Not that he's ever been anything but wonderful since our divorce.

I head into the house and call out to Michael and Olivia.

Michael calls back. I don't really want to have this conversation with him here.

"In the living room!" he says.

I round the corner to find the two of them on the couch, playing one of Olivia's games. From the action on the screen, it looks like they're playing some kind of war game. The two of them faced off against each other, their avatars taking up either half of the screen.

"We're hunting for each other," Olivia says after I've been staring at the screen for a moment.

"Oh, that's nice," I say with a forced laugh.

It's just then that Olivia rounds a corner and shoots her dad in the head.

"YES!" she exclaims.

"Dammit!" Michael says, tossing the remote beside him. "I haven't won one yet."

"Olivia," I say. "Could I talk to you for a minute? In private?"

Olivia looks up from the game, alarm on her features. Me wanting to talk to her without her dad is a big deal. I don't want him there when I ask her. She might be too afraid of his reaction to tell me the truth.

I motion for her to come out back with me, and she does. We slip out the sliding glass doors and I walk over to the pool. I sit and dangle my legs in. I invite her to do the same.

"Olivia," I say. "I have to ask you something really important that might make you feel uncomfortable. It might seem like you should lie, but I need you to tell the truth. Do you understand me?" I ask, looking into her eyes.

She just nods. I watch as she swallows, clearly nervous.

"Did Billy ever touch you in a way that made you feel weird?" I ask.

"What?" Olivia asks. Her face flushes. I see the color change under the patio lights just behind us. She's embarrassed. "No. God, no."

"Olivia, I need you to be honest if he did," I say.

"Mom, no!" she says loudly. "He never did anything like that."

I look at her, not sure if I trust what she's saying.

"If you change your mind, you can tell me later," I assure her. "If you're not ready to talk about it, that's okay," I tell her, grabbing both of her hands.

She looks at me like I'm a crazy person. Like she has no intention of ever telling me anything about what I asked or about anything ever again.

"I love you," I say.

"I love you, too, mom," she says.

I get up and help her get up with me. We head back inside.

I SIT down with my glass and sip it. They play another round like the one they were playing before I interrupted and when Michael loses again, they decide to switch to a racing game. It reminds me of the kind that you could play at pizza places back in the nineties.

Except the graphics are about a million times better now.

I get up and have a second glass. Michael looks over at me, his eyes lingering on the glass as if to ask me if that's my second. He looks at me like he wants to know what I was asking Olivia, too.

I shoot him a look that doesn't invite further commentary. He turns his focus back to the game.

I sit idly by while they play their game, letting myself get lost in fantasy again. I think about how things might have been. But then my mind drifts to Jackie and what happened here today. It feels like a lifetime ago, already. The encounter with Lindsay totally removed me from dealing with the feelings it brought up. But now, cradled in the security of the past and my second glass of wine, they start to surface.

I've been attracted to Jackie since I first met her. Not just physically, but more than that. Romantically. Our friendship was always closer. Far closer than the friendships I had with Amanda and Nicole, even though we were good friends, too.

I think back on other female friendships I had that burned a little too brightly.

I think about how things had always been simmering between me and Jackie. At the parties, it was like, even though the guys were watching, we retreated into our own little world. It wasn't for the male gaze. It was for us. And then, today, when it really was just about us, it was explosive.

My heart quickens at the thought of her even now.

But it plummets with the idea that she'll never leave Nathan. It's not like that for her.

And besides, it would never work. Jackie lied to me.

Jackie is so much younger than me. The idea of her might be intoxicating, but I don't know what the reality holds aside from being her friend all these years. Being someone's friend is a hell of a lot easier than being their lover and living with them day in and day out.

The thoughts overwhelm me.

I try to focus back on what Olivia and Michael are up to on the screen. They laugh and he teases her. She teases him back, giving as good as she gets. I feel a stabbing pain thinking about her having to go back to school, eventually. Sooner rather than later. I can't home school her. Her tuition is paid through Christmas, when they get one of their big breaks. Maybe it's for the best, her transferring to public school.

Maybe the rumors haven't traveled that far.

One can hope.

I sigh and nestle back into my chair.

THIRTY-SIX

I WATCH them play video games for hours. I watch Olivia's face for any micro expression that might tell me she was lying earlier and really wants to tell me what her step-dad might have done to her. But it's like the conversation never happened. She and her dad carry on until midnight, laughing and teasing each other, even including me in the fun.

Finally, I tell Olivia she needs to hang it up for the evening.

She groans, looking over at her dad.

"You heard your mom, kiddo," he says. He looks over at me, resting his elbow on the back of the couch and pressing his fist to his cheek. He smiles and winks at me, letting me know he has my back.

It's another one of those moments that I want to bottle up. Save for later. A moment that reminds me of when things were good in the past.

I look at him for a moment as he watches Olivia gather up her gaming system to take back into her bedroom. Michael's always been handsome to me. He still is. Maybe even more so now, after everything he's been there for us through.

Olivia disappears down the hallway and closes her door behind her.

I sit in my chair by the couch and Michael stays where he is, too. The room is quiet.

"Like old times, huh?" he asks.

"We might have been arguing," I tell him with a sad laugh.

I run my finger around the rim of the wineglass.

I stand up and walk over to the couch. Michael looks surprised. I sit down beside him and he resituates himself, removing his arm from the back of the couch.

"No, keep it there," I tell him.

He's silent, letting his arm fall around my shoulders.

"Just hold me," I tell him softly. I take a sip of my wine.

Michael cautiously pulls me closer to him. I feel his heart beating through his gray t-shirt. It's pounding a million miles a minute. I snuggle against him, instantly comforted by the feeling of his body against mine.

I sigh contentedly, and Michael relaxes a little.

We sit there for a moment, adjusting to this. Both of us trying to get comfortable touching the other like this for the first time in years.

I lean my head over onto his shoulder. And I feel him press his lips to my hair and kiss me on top of the head.

"I miss this sometimes," I whisper into the air between us.

"Me, too," Michael whispers into my hair. His words

are slow, heavy. Like he's waited for this and the words have gathered weight in all that time.

He squeezes my arm and kisses my hair again.

I tilt my face up to his.

Michael looks down at me, his eyes searching my face for some clear signal. He looks frantic and I feel his heart beat faster again.

"Just kiss me, you fool," I tell him with a grin.

And that's all it takes.

Michael kisses me with all the force of years of pent up need. His mouth covers mine, his breath fans across my cheeks. He pulls me on top of him and I drop my wine glass onto the carpet. I don't care.

I straddle him and he pulls my face down to meet his, kissing me like he's wanted to do it every day since we separated.

His kiss is comfort. It's all things familiar and safe.

He runs his hands through my hair. I reach for the buckle of his belt and undo it. I stand up long enough for him to shed his jeans and I pull him by the hand toward the bedroom. He grabs his jeans at his feet and doesn't hesitate. He follows me back into the bed. He pulls his boxers down and when I look at him, he's more than ready.

He strips me of my shirt and my shorts. I crawl on top of him.

He wraps his arms around me and cradles me as we fuck. It's slow, our eyes locked together. I feel like my soul is reaching out and touching his. His reaches back and they dance in the exhaled breath between us.

Him inside me feels like I've come home.

It feels like safety.

And it feels like everything I need right now.

The edges of my vision blur as my body becomes aware of its every inch. Finally, Michael flips me over and pulls my hips to the edge of the bed. He snakes an arm under each thigh and presses his mouth against me at my most vulnerable place.

I gasp, the sensation overwhelming me, drowning me in waves of pleasure.

Michael kisses me there, just as needfully as he kissed me on the couch. He makes love to me with his mouth, saying all the things we've left unspoken between each other for years. I pant and then cry out, only remembering at the last moment to stifle it with a fist.

Michael slows his kisses, but doesn't stop. I squirm beneath him, but he's not done. Finally, he sits up and makes eye contact with me.

"Fuck, Kim," he groans. He climbs on top of me and pulls me into his embrace, both of us lying side by side on the bed. "You taste just like I remember," he groans into my ear.

He pulls me into him, and we have sex.

Afterwards, I fall asleep in his arms.

IN THE MORNING, Michael kisses me before he darts out the door, not wanting Olivia to know we spent the night together. That's the last thing she needs.

He wraps his arms around me and hugs me tight before releasing me.

"I need to go," he whispers.

"Yeah," I say, still in the haze of what happened last night. For now, I'm fantasizing about the comforts of what I know. And the possibility that, after the traumatic school bullying episode Olivia experienced, maybe I'm ready to settle down.

Part of me knows this is all false hope, though.

I know who I am at my core.

Michael knows that, too. But he's so happy. I can't help but feel like I've led him on. Like he thinks this is going to continue.

I don't have the emotional energy to end it now. It can wait.

He slips out the door and I watch it close behind him, hoping that I haven't done irreparable damage to our relationship.

THIRTY-SEVEN

THE MORNING IS like any other.

I head into Olivia's room to see if she wants to talk after last night. I feel like she's going to be able to tell that her dad stayed here.

She's busy getting ready to take a shower, though, seemingly none the worse for wear over the whole thing.

"Good morning," I tell her.

"Good morning, mom," she says, sounding more chipper than I expected.

Olivia disappears into the bathroom. She doesn't shut the door all the way. A remnant of her childhood. She was afraid there was a shark that lived in the drain below the house and that it could get you if you weren't careful in the shower. She also thought the shark lived in the pool, too.

The thought makes me sad. She still wants my protection. Something that I didn't give her when she was at school. Instead, I'd been selfish.

I hear the sound of the water running. After a

minute or two, I hear Olivia step into the shower. I busy myself looking around her room, really taking it in for the first time in ages. I look at the posters on her wall. Boy bands that she swears she's outgrown but never bothered to remove their images from her walls. Quotes from her favorite television series. Basketball awards. A WNBA poster. Cut outs from magazines. It's really not that different from my room when I was her age. Though I never got to stay in one place for very long.

The thought of telling Olivia we have to move comes back to me. I'm just waiting for the news about Billy's firm. It's devastating. Any strength I had left is sucked out of me by that notion.

Our lives are about to change. I know that much is true. I also know that I'm a survivor. And Olivia takes after me in so many ways. Why not that one, too? Not that any child should have to be a survivor. But the harsh truth of life is that it asks that of all of us at some point. Some more often than others. Some relentlessly.

I hope this is the only thing Olivia ever has to survive.

I breathe in the scent of her shower gel. Something fruity from the bath and body store down the street. Maybe I'll take her shopping as soon as I get some extra money. Try to give her back some normalcy.

The idea of moving to the beach comes back to me. And it's right around then that my phone rings.

It's Michael.

Just a smiley face emoji.

It makes me want to throw up. I'm a horrible person.

I force it to the back of my mind. I think about everything that happened that night. All of it seems like a blur now. I don't know what to make of the entire situation.

I think about what Billy must have been carrying.

Not for the first time, I wonder if he killed himself.

My mind drifts for a moment into nothingness. I just stare into space, and for the first time since this whole thing started, I let myself relax.

OLIVIA SHOWERS FOREVER. I stay in her room, waiting for her to get out. Once, I peek in the bathroom just to make sure her figure is upright under the water and not crumpled in a heap. Sometimes she takes so long that I'm afraid her shark has eaten her after all. Satisfied that she's alive, I go back to sit on her bed.

When I do, the bed creaks under my weight.

And something rattles.

I stand up and sit down again, thinking there might be something wrong with the springs in her bed. Another thing to have to worry about now that we don't have any money. I sit back down and the bed makes the same noise. It's faint, but I definitely heard it.

"Shit," I mutter.

I get down on my knees and start to feel around beneath the bed, expecting to find something loose. Maybe it's the frame itself. We could get her a new bed frame pretty cheaply.

I reach beneath it, and my hand comes in contact with plastic. A bag.

I furrow my brow.

It's tucked, hanging from one of the slats. I lift the mattress slightly and release it. I pull a zipping plastic bag from beneath the bed. Inside it are four white tablets. I stare at the bag for a second.

I reach back under the bed, thinking that I felt something else. And I did. My hand is met by the sharp edge of a plastic cover on a notebook. I pull it out. It's hot pink, see through. There's nothing written on the first page.

I put the bag on the floor and open the notebook.

There are journal entries in it. The first chronicles Olivia's first day back at school after Christmas last year. They're the usual teen fare. One of them is about someone she has a crush on. I smile as I read it. It's so innocent.

I keep going, getting lost in her words. In the way she sees the world.

Another entry is about the play she was in last spring. There are about twelve more after it about day-to-day things.

Then I read the next entry. And I have to read the words twice to make sure I understood them.

He snuck into my bedroom again last night. He told me he would stop, but he hasn't.

I stare at the final words of the entry, trying to process them. Was there some boy I didn't know about? Had he snuck into our house?

I go on.

The next entry is worse. She details an assault. I clap my hand to my mouth and read it again, wishing that I had misinterpreted it the first time. A tear streaks down my face. I think of what Lindsay told me. All the dots connect so quickly.

This is Olivia's account of a sexual assault. A rape.

I can't stop reading even though I should.

I got the stuff today.

My eyes dart to the pills in the baggie on the nightstand.

My heart starts beating faster.

He had it coming. He deserved it. No one protected me from him. Billy Karlsen is a rapist and a pedophile.

I drop the notebook.

I don't notice the figure in the doorway.

"Mom?" Olivia's voice is small, timid.

I look over at her. She sees the pills. She sees the notebook.

She knows I know.

She looks at me blankly.

"Were you looking through my things?" she asks.

"Olivia," I say, standing up and rushing to her.

She's stiff.

"It's okay," I assure her. "It's okay. Okay?"

I pull away, and she looks numb. She's silent.

"Olivia," I breathe. I'm sobbing now, too. "Why didn't you tell me?"

"Tell you what?" she says into my ear.

"That Billy hurt you!" I scream. "I would have helped you! I *will* help you! No one ever has to know about this."

Olivia looks bewildered. But panic rises to the forefront.

"I'm going to make sure nothing happens to you," I tell her.

"What's going to happen?" she asks, frantic.

"Baby, I'm going to protect you," I tell her.

I realize the irony in what I'm saying. But this time, I'm going to do whatever is necessary.

Just then, there's a knock at the door.

THIRTY-EIGHT

I LOOK out of Olivia's bedroom window and see Underwood's car.

"Shit," I mutter. "Keep these in here," I tell her, handing her the pills and the journal. "Just stay in here and don't come out."

She nods her head furiously.

I head out of her room. My heart pounds as I open the door. I put on my best smile for Underwood.

"How can I help you, Detective?" I ask.

Underwood eyes me for a moment.

"Good morning, Mrs. Karlsen," he says. He steps inside without asking. "I was just coming by to check on you. I noticed that your ex-husband stayed over last night," he says.

"You were watching me?" I ask, taken aback. "Why the hell were you spying on me?"

"Oh, it's not spying," he says, brushing away my concern. "No hard feelings. It's my job to see what you're up to."

"Is that why you're here?" I ask.

He walks around the living room, looking at different things on the shelves.

"I suppose," he says. "Or to give you one last chance to tell me what really happened that night," he adds.

I stare at him, flabbergasted.

I don't know what to say.

"I don't know what happened," I tell him for the millionth time.

"Someone does," he says. "And if you don't know what happened, I bet you know who *does*."

My heart flutters in my chest. The idea that danger is this close to my child. That this is my one chance to prevent it from coming for her. It fills me with dread, nausea, the sensation that I'm floating above my own body. It's ten million times more terrifying than the night that Billy died.

I stand there, letting it sink in for a moment. My husband was a predator in every sense of the word. He hurt me. He hurt my friend. He hurt my *child*. I allowed him to hurt my child.

"You can tell me the truth, Kimberly," he says.

He turns to face me then.

"I've told you the truth," I tell him. My voice is meek, more quiet than I mean for it to be. I clear my throat. "I've already told you," I say.

"Do you mind if I have one last look around the house?" Underwood asks.

His tone is pleasant. My gut clenches.

"No problem," I say, not sounding like myself. "Olivia's asleep," I tell him. "Just don't disturb her."

But just then, Olivia pokes her head out of the hallway.

"Is everything okay?" she asks.

My heart almost drops out of my body into the depths of hell.

"Everything's fine, sweetie. You can go back and finish your nap," I tell her.

"Were you taking a nap?" Underwood asks her.

She shakes her head.

My heart beats faster.

"Your mom said you were taking a nap," Underwood says.

"I just took a shower," Olivia says.

"Do you mind if I have a look in your room, Olivia?" Underwood says.

Olivia's eyes dart to mine. She's scared.

"No," she says.

Before I can stop Underwood, he's down the hall into her room. I grab Olivia, drawing her body into mine.

I don't know what to do. I don't know what I *can* do.

I could kill him, I think.

I could kill him right now and we could dispose of his body.

And then run away.

I hold her tight, not daring to make a move. I'm paralyzed by fear.

Underwood's gone for what seems like an eternity. Finally, he emerges.

And in his hand, I see the two things I hoped I wouldn't.

He's placed each of them in an evidence bag.

"Olivia," he says softly.

She looks up at him.

"Olivia Williams," he repeats her name. "You're under arrest for the murder of William Karlsen."

Olivia clings to me. I fight him. I kick and scream and he calls for backup. He cuffs me at the wrists and ankles and sits me on the couch. I throw my body off as I watch him cuff Olivia. He takes her outside and puts her in the back of his car. The whole time, she screams out *"Mom! Mom!" until her voice is a rasp.*

I scream for her. I bawl.

I'm incoherent.

Other officers arrive at the house. Michael arrives.

I guess they called him.

They explain the situation to him. He holds me.

The world is collapsing in on me. I'm being sucked into the void.

Michael rocks me back and forth. The cops search the house again.

They leave.

Michael stays.

And then I faint.

I WAKE UP IN BED. Michael is holding my hand. Everyone's gone.

I shoot out of bed the moment I realize where I am. I struggle to put on my shoes.

"We have to go," I say.

"It's okay," he tells me, reaching for me.

He's too calm.

"What's wrong with you?! We have to go! Now!"

"Olivia's here," he says.

"What? How?" I ask.

"I bailed her out of jail. They agreed to put her on house arrest until this is over."

"Until what is over?" I ask.

"The trial, Kim," Michael says somberly.

It all rushes back over me. The whole thing. Olivia killed her step-father and I couldn't shield her from the repercussions. I wasn't big enough, strong enough. I didn't have the courage.

"I should have killed Underwood," I sob.

"Kim," Michael tries to speak reason to me.

"I should have killed him and we should have run away," I tell him.

"No jury will convict her," he says. "And if they do, there's no way they're going to send her to prison for long," he adds. "I already got her a lawyer. The best I can afford," he adds. "That's what he told me."

"He doesn't think it's likely that she'll be convicted?" I ask through tears.

"Not of murder," he says. "It's going to be okay. I'm here for both of you," he tells me.

I collect myself and go check on Olivia.

THIRTY-NINE

THE NEXT FEW months feel like years.

She maintains her innocence, swearing she didn't do it and has no idea who did. Trauma psychologists tell us it's normal for a girl to behave this way in such a situation. In fact, they argue, it's going to help her case. And in the end, they're right.

Olivia is convicted of manslaughter and, given the circumstances, she's sentenced to 8 months in a psychiatric facility for minors.

It's the best we could have hoped for.

I lost the house and all my possessions and still no one knows where the money went. At first everyone thought it had to be bad investments. Eventually, it couldn't be proven. He was taking out large amounts of cash and it just vanished. Maybe he intended to leave us. Whatever it was, we lost the house. Michael graciously took me in, and we gingerly tiptoed around our new relationship for the next half of a year.

And after an eternity separated from my child, the day arrives when Olivia is getting out.

We pick her up at the facility and when she comes out, they have plucked all the light from her eyes. My stomach drops. I run to her, wrapping her in an embrace.

"Baby," I whisper.

"Mom, I love you," she sobs into my hair.

I squeeze her even tighter. Michael wraps both of us in his arms.

"My girls," he whispers, and I'm not sure he even realizes that he said it.

And for the first time in a year, I feel safe.

WHEN I GET into the truck, I climb into the back seat. I want to be as close to Olivia as I can be. I'm never leaving her side again.

Michael drives us to his house. We sit down for our first family dinner in about a year.

I make fettuccini. One of Olivia's favorites. I make shrimp and chicken both, telling them Michael and Olivia they can choose which meat they'd prefer. I go all out. Salad, mozzarella sticks, the works. The two of them gobble it down like they've never seen food before in their lives.

"I'm so glad that it turned out the way it did," Michael says of everything we've been through in the past year.

I sigh, enjoying my food.

"I am, too," I say.

I glance at Olivia.

She smiles at me. I see a glimpse of the girl she used to be. For a brief second, I could swear it was like nothing ever happened. Although, I know that's not the case. Olivia needs therapy.

I feel like a pitiful excuse for a mom.

Still, with all of us together, it feels like something safe. Something like normal.

Maybe we could all adjust to this.

I look at Michael and see the happiness on his face when he looks at Olivia.

She smiles back at him. They've always been in each other's back pocket. Best friends, if father and daughter ever could be. I think Michael would do anything for Olivia.

I think we both would.

After dinner, Olivia clears her throat at the table. It's clear she has something she wants to talk about. I glance at her.

"I've been thinking," Olivia says to both of us. Michael chances a glance at me. He winks. He always gets a kick out of any time that Olivia says or does something much better suited to an adult. He always has. It makes me smile despite myself. I turn my focus back on her.

"What have you been thinking?" Michael asks her.

"What if we all moved to the beach?" There's a flicker of hope in her eyes. A lot is riding on this for her.

I sigh and look at Michael. He can't very well up and leave his job here. He has a mortgage, too. There's something mischievous in his eyes though. Like he's actually considering the thought of moving. All of us. Somewhere new.

For a moment, I let it dance through my mind. The idea of starting over. Olivia wouldn't have those kids gnawing at her. We'd all be free of the rumor mill. A fresh start might be good, not just for Olivia, but me, too.

And it would be good if we went together. I like the idea.

I giggle.

"You're not actually—" I look at Michael. "Are you thinking about it?"

"You look like you're thinking about it," he says with a grin.

I toss my napkin at him. He bats it away.

"What do you say?" Michael asks.

Olivia is brimming with excitement. I look at her.

And that's all it takes.

FORTY

BY FALL MICHAEL has talked me into a house in Port Aransas that boasts two master bedrooms.

We can all be together. It's the best thing possible for us, he says.

I drag my feet on making a decision. I don't want to send the wrong message. But the idea of Olivia having stability and the three of us really being as close to a happy family as we can be is appealing. Especially after everything she's gone through.

He buys the house.

By Halloween, I'm curled up on a modern sofa in the giant living room of our new shared space. Michael and I haven't really defined what's happening between us, but I'd be a liar if I said I wasn't enjoying it. I have a cup of hot apple cider in my hands, and Michael and Olivia are at the beach, even though there's a slight chill in the air.

I flip through our streaming services and land on Hulu. I pick a Halloween movie, something I know Olivia likes, so it'll be playing when they get back. I've been carefully curating her existence here, trying to make everything an experience for her to look back on fondly. All of it in the hopes that I can erase some of the pain she felt at Billy's hand.

Olivia is flourishing.

Michael is, too. And I'm not far behind.

I think the guilt will always eat at me, though.

I watch the beginning of the movie and make quick work of the apple cider. I head to the bedroom to grab a gift basket I made for each of them for Halloween. Both of them include candy, shower gel, and gift cards for the video game store.

I take them out into the kitchen and set them on the bar. I tug at the ribbons, making sure they're just right.

I remember one other thing I got for the baskets. A gift card for each of their favorite restaurants. I picked it up today and forgot to stick it in the baskets. I head for the bedroom again.

As I pass by the study, something catches my eye.

A statue at an odd angle, catching lamplight. It normally doesn't do that.

I stop and head into the room. A book next to it is slightly out of place, pushed in slightly farther than it normally is.

I reach up for it, meaning to just pull it back out, but when I pull it forward, it tumbles to the floor and a series of papers fall out. All of them worn notebook pages. I start to gather them, figuring it's some kind of an old journal of Michael's. Then something catches my eye on one of the pages.

For you, after I'm gone

Jesus Christ. Is this some sort of package for me in case Michael dies? I know I shouldn't look, but I do. But the papers that follow look like a series of notes.

Usually in his office 6:45-10:00 pm
Party Friday night; Olivia with me

I read the words a couple of times, trying to make sense of them.

Then I turn over another page. It's a floor plan of the house I lived in with Billy, purchased from a home builder. The same builder that we used. I see his logo in the corner of the printout.

I swallow, but my mouth feels dry.

I turn over another piece of paper.

Rohypnol

My gut clenches, my heart beats faster.

Beneath the drug name is the name of the website it was ordered from.

I turn over one more page.

I read the words.

It's the draft of one of Olivia's journal entries. There's a note at the bottom.

What will do the most to convince Kim?

A picture of Lindsay falls out as I shuffle the papers.

I pick up more pieces, each one giving me a clearer, more damning picture of our perfect life.

Finally, I come to one about Olivia.

Olivia will be fine; only a few months likely

On the next page is a letter.

Dear Kim,

If you're reading this, I'm gone and I've left this for you.

I don't even know how to begin to tell you how much I love you. You're everything to me. And I've known it since the moment I met you. I'm so glad things worked out the way they did.

I worked on this for a long time. And I did it all for you.

Kim, we're meant to be in each other's lives. The night we made love after Billy died, I knew I'd made the right choice.

I waited for the right time. I knew he was treating you badly. And I had a private investigator look into him. He found Lindsay and I got in touch with her. It turned out that Billy had molested her when she was a kid, but Lindsay was small. Under 10. She told me Olivia wasn't in his age range. I used this to my advantage.

Anonymously, I wrote to him. I told him I knew about this. And that if he ever touched Olivia, I'd kill him in broad daylight. I made a deal with Lindsay. I'd blackmail him and she'd get part of the money if she contacted you and shared this information. I told her that you'd take it better coming from her than from me. You might have been mad if I had told you.

I piled the money up, saving it for you guys. I kept an eye on Olivia, making sure she was safe. And then I bought the Rohypnol. I used a website on the dark web. It was all anonymous. I walked from my house to the house just behind yours. I jumped the fence and snuck in with my key to Billy's office. I put a bunch of the pills in his whiskey. I knew he never shared. And then I waited.

I came back that night. The night of the party, and I watched from the dark side of the yard as he fell unconscious. I dragged him out of the office and into the pool, leaving him there.

I knew they'd never be able to pin it on you because there wasn't sufficient evidence. I was careful with the scene. Wore gloves, the whole nine yards.

I wrote the diary that I put under Olivia's bed with the pills. I knew that the system would go easy on her given the circumstances. And Olivia's a tough kid. Plus, *one time she told me she'd do anything to have us all back together again.*

I guess I put that to the test.

If you're reading this, I'm probably gone. I'm intending to save it and keep it safe until one day when I know it's time.

I just want you to know that I would move heaven and earth for you. I knew you were unhappy. And there's nothing in this world stronger than the bond I have with you. I'll never forget the look in your eyes that night when I knew.

I love you more than any other person on this earth, Kim.

Love,
Michael

The world spins around me. Is this possible? This is insane. I think of little moments along the way that led us here. I remember a time in a gas station on our way down when Michael got me my favorite candy bar without prompting. How he brings me gifts all the time. How he used to do that back in Dallas, too. He always remained ingrained in our lives.

He orchestrated everything.

He put his daughter up for a murder he committed.

She spent almost a year in a psych ward.

Michael blackmailed Billy and took our money. He planted evidence in his daughter's room.

I don't know this man.

The entire last six months of my life have been a lie.

And Billy's murderer lives under the same roof as me now.

My heart stops.

And then I hear the back door open.

"Hey!" Michael calls. "We're back, honey!"

ACKNOWLEDGMENTS

I would be remiss if I didn't give a huge thank you to the Psychological Thriller Readers group on Facebook. Y'all encouraged me right away to stay on top of this project. I was blown away by your support, and I hope I delivered.

To my editor, Collette Carmon, for always keeping my 'ands' and 'buts' in check and making this manuscript the strongest it could be.

To Katie and Johnetta, thank you for always being my rocks when it comes to the indie publishing world.

To my family, thank you for all your support and all the little celebrations along the way.

To my dogs, who were at my feet throughout the entire process with this one.

And thank you to my mom. I couldn't have done it without you. As always.

Now, on to the next one!

ABOUT THE AUTHOR

I started writing when I was 7. The book was called *It Came Floating Up*. It was inspired by many trips to the beach and watching a few too many episodes of *The X-Files* with my grandmother. The book was about a monster lurking in the sargasso seaweed just off the coast of Corpus Christi. In the dedication, I wrote:

To my family, who has been there through everything.

I was 7. If only I'd known then what exactly *everything* would entail.

Since then, I've only gotten more dramatic and more obsessed with *The X-Files* and storytelling.

My books all have one thing in common: they are inspired by some element of truth either in my own life or something I pick out of a headline or a history book. Mostly, though, my writing is inspired by my own experiences and emotions, just blown up on a grander scale with a murder or two to make it exciting.

Just call me the Taylor Swift of psychological thrillers.

JOIN THE MARNIE WRITES THRILLERS NEWSLETTER

Get updates, freebies, news about me and my dogs, and more!

www.marniewritesthrillers.com/novella-sign-up

ALSO BY MARNIE VINGE

PSYCHOLOGICAL THRILLERS

The Getaway

For Rosie